DAVID[illegible]

MEMOIRS

DAVID CROSBIE'S MEMOIRS

Adapted from
Phil Redmond's Brookside
by
Rachel Braverman

BOXTREE

The publishers would like to thank Phil Redmond, Alexis Redmond and Mal Young for their help and advice in producing this book.

First published in the UK in 1995 by Boxtree Limited, Broadwall House, 21 Broadwall, London, SE1 9PL

ISBN 0 7522 0172 7

10 9 8 7 6 5 4 3 2 1

A CIP catalogue entry for this book is available from the British Library

Typeset by SX Composing, Rayleigh, Essex
Printed in Great Britain by
Cox & Wyman Ltd., Reading, Berkshire

Introduction

Ever since I was a lad, it has been my ambition to write my memoirs. From the age of eleven, I have kept a journal to record the important happenings in my life. In this, I am following a noble tradition as I am sure you, the discerning reader, will know. One has only to think of Samuel Pepys' classic description of the Fire of London, the Churchill Papers and Alan Clarke's recent political exposé.

The time is now ripe for me to publish. To go public. Jean, my good lady, is inclined to scoff at my literary aspirations. Unfortunately, she often fails to take my position as seriously as she ought. No doubt she will change her tune when the broadsheets publish their reviews and the British Library are begging for copies.

My credentials are, frankly, impeccable. As founder and Chairman of the Brookside Residents' Association (hereinafter known as the B.R.A.), I am the official voice of the people. Although I only moved here a few years ago, I am absolutely at the heart of the community.

I well remember my first meeting with Ron Dixon, my neighbour, very good friend and proprietor of local emporium, *The Trading Post*. Max Farnham, husband to my daughter Patricia, introduced us.

'Bet your friends call you 'Bing',' said Ron.

To be absolutely honest, the reference escaped me for some minutes. I thought it could be some local code. However, when I cottoned on, I was tickled pink to be compared to the old crooner (and I play a mean round of golf myself!). It was my first example of the famous Scouse sense of humour. As I laughed, I remember seeing a welcoming look of satisfaction spread across Ron's face. I realized later that I'd passed the Liverpool test of acceptance. By allowing myself to be ribbed, I had proved I was a decent chap.

But I digress – back to the matter in hand. I have chosen to publish the 1995 volume of my scribblings, as I believe it to have been a most extraordinary period in my life, or anyone else's for that matter.

It's a tale of murder, mystery and intrigue. We have had to cope with the hounds of Fleet Street, the chickens of Casa Bevron and the downright abominations of Jimmy Corkhill and his sidekick, Cracker. We have experienced fame and even fortune. I have lived life on the 'cutting edge' – to use a trendy phrase. The truth about these extraordinary events, and more besides, is laid before you in the following pages.

Now read on, dear reader, whilst I await my phone calls from *Question Time* and dear old Melvyn Bragg . . .

30th January 1995

A most extraordinary day.

It started well, even triumphantly. After weeks of campaigning against Jimmy Corkhill and his wretched pooch, the council has finally agreed to put up a notice. The lamp-post outside my front door now declares that any canine caught fouling the footpath renders its owners liable to a fine of up to £500. Perhaps it will teach that carbuncle on the face of society to train his dog in basic hygiene. Fancy calling a dog 'Cracker' in any case. Ridiculous name, even if it did first appear at Christmas.

I was inspecting the council's handiwork with Max when we noticed a commotion outside number 10's front door. The local constabulary were there and I noticed Rosie and Eddie Banks from number 9 talking to them. Even from across the road, I could see Rosie looked quite upset.

I was somewhat unnerved myself, as I hadn't seen Mrs Mandy Jordache or her daughters, Beth and Rachel, for a few days. Immediately, my thoughts turned to Corkhill. Experience has taught me always to expect the worst when that man's around. I haven't forgotten his little episode of burglary. He proved to be responsible for a series of break-ins on the Close, including the invasion of my daughter's house. The months that miscreant spent behind bars were a positive reprieve. How he has the audacity to hang around here, I don't know. It wouldn't surprise me if we discover he's at the centre of some nefarious wrong-doing.

As members of the residents association assisting our local constabulary, it was clearly my duty and Max's to investigate what was going on. What we were about to discover changed this community for ever. Eddie Banks' garden has been subject to severe flooding over the past weeks. He turned the entire area into a sea of mud, but failed to locate the source of the problem. In desperation, he, Rosie and Jimmy Corkhill started digging under the Jordaches' patio. Normally, I would deplore undertaking such actions without permission, but the Jordaches went AWOL so suddenly the Bankses didn't have a chance to talk to them.

About three flagstones in, Eddie's spade struck an obstacle. He investigated immediately. Apparently, Sinbad, our local window cleaner and consort to Mrs Jordache, had some kind of a stash buried there, which he was anxious to keep from prying eyes. Whatever it was, it can't have been anything like the hideous object that was about to be revealed.

Jumping into the hole, Eddie discovered a parcel wrapped in a black plastic bin-liner. Gingerly, he tore open a small corner, whilst Rosie and Corkhill stood by with baited breath. As soon as he broke the seal, an unbearable stench hit the air. Eddie peeled back a bit more of the plastic.

Suddenly, he gave a yell of pure terror. The wrapping fell away to reveal what appeared to be a hand. No, more than that, it *was* a hand. Rosie and Corkhill fell back in alarm and the three of them ended up flailing in the mud. One can only imagine the sheer horror of actually touching the cold, dank flesh of a corpse. Eddie is normally the bravest of fellows, but he was reduced to a gibbering wreck. Poor Rosie practically had hysterics.

Corkhill's immediate reaction was naturally to try and cover up any potential wrongdoing. That man has absolutely no conscience whatsoever. Naturally, the Bankses refused to go along with any of his dirty dealings. It wouldn't surprise me if Corkhill himself didn't have something to do with the gruesome find.

The boys in blue arrived minutes later with blaring sirens and flashing lights. As we watched, a second police car and a van from the Mersey Force Scientific Support Unit drew up. One lad started unravelling yellow tape, literally wrapping the house up. No one can go in and no one can come out without permission. They're probably going over the place with a fine tooth comb even now, searching for clues.

The Bankses, Max and I put our heads together to go over events of recent days. Mandy and Rachel Jordache only came back from a holiday in Ireland a couple of weeks ago. Sinbad, our local window cleaner and consort to Mrs Jordache, had been away with them. God knows where young Beth had been. Staying with one of her disreputable medical student friends, no doubt.

No sooner had they all returned home, than they were gone again. Without a word to anyone. In fact, Rachel had arranged a surprise birthday party for Sinbad on the very evening they vanished. The guests duly arrived, but the hosts failed to appear. Very Agatha Christie.

It's hard to believe our neighbours could be mixed up in anything underhand. The Jordaches have been residents of the Close for a couple of years now. Mandy Jordache is even secretary of the B.R.A. Admittedly, young Beth's lifestyle leaves a lot to be desired, in my opinion. No matter what Jean and Patsy say, a so-called lesbian lifestyle is not natural. However, even I recognize it's hardly an indication of criminal tendencies.

As for Sinbad, he's the salt of the earth. Always willing to lend a hand and marvellous for Mandy. After all that her wretched husband put her through, she's really perked up.

Surely, Mandy and the girls know nothing about this. Whatever's down there could have been buried years ago, long before they came here. Speculation is rife.

On the other hand, a ghastly discovery like this *and* the inhabitants' disappearance looks like more than mere coincidence. It all points to some kind of skullduggery. The plot thickens . . .

31st January 1995

Number 10 looks like it's under siege. A yellow canopy has been built over the patio. Two men in blue protective suits have been digging up the garden. Their hoods were drawn right up over their heads and they were wearing overshoes. One can only shudder to think what they expect to find.

Of course, the story has been leaked to the press.

Journalists have been swarming all over the place, like flies attracted to the product of Corkhill's Cracker.

Speaking of whom, Jean and I were walking in the Close and we caught both master and dog acting in a most reprehensible manner. Cracker was actually doing her business directly under my notice, whilst Corkhill gawped cheerily at the police activity. He had the gall to greet me with 'Good turn out, kids'.

I hardly think a tragic event like this should be treated as a spectator sport. I proceeded to remonstrate with him re Cracker and to draw his attention to the new sign.

'Cracker's an intelligent dog,' Corkhill smirked. 'But reading is not one of her talents.' The man is an ink-blot on the map of civilised society.

Jean reminded him of the dangers to children, but he was completely blasé. Called it 'marking out her territory'. For sheer effrontery, the man's next remarks will take some beating.

'Anyway,' he said. 'I'm only here to see if those journos are interested in my story.'

'You're not going to talk to the press, are you?' Jean protested.

'Why not? I used to live there, didn't I?'

True enough. His brother, I believe by the name of Billy, owned the house before the Jordaches moved in. Whenever Jimmy's wife, Jackie, saw sense and threw him out, he used to impose on his long-suffering relatives.

I glanced across the road and saw that there must be

some thirty journalists hanging about, looking as if they're digging in for the duration. There was only one thing for it. I summoned an emergency meeting of the B.R.A.

Ron and Beverley from number 8 were our hosts. I made a slight gaff by referring to them as 'the Dixons'. It's so hard to know how to refer to a couple who haven't actually got round to tying the knot. I imagine that they will if and when Ron can persuade his wife to divorce him. But that's modern day living for you. A complete loss of morals, if you ask me. As Beverley only moved in a few weeks ago, I haven't got used to the idea of her being in residence. Trouble is, I ended up by reminding myself – and everyone else, presumably – of their recent scandal. Ron is so very much the middle-aged small business type and Beverley, frankly, always looks as if she's got up for the local discotheque. Looking at them side by side on the sofa, with baby Josh in between them, they seem to be generations apart, not merely separated by some twenty years.

Max and Patricia have rather taken against them. The Farnham moniker for them is 'The Clampitts'. I believe this is to imply their social standing. Personally, I wouldn't label my house Casa Bevron, but each to their own. Bev's a nice, friendly cheerful sort of girl, devoted to Josh and Ron and making great efforts to belong. Ron has always done his fair share re the residents' association, so I, for one, am not about to turn the cold shoulder. He even offered me a temporary roof when Jean and I were not seeing eye to eye.

The meeting got off on the wrong foot. Rosie and Eddie were there and were questioned closely as to precisely what happened when they made their unpleasant find. We do know that, along with the mystery hand, a whole body has now been exhumed, but no identification has been released. Ron thought it could be a German paratrooper from the war. Of course, this was dismissed when Ron's son, Michael, pointed out that the luckless soldier would have also had to have wrapped himself up in bin bags! The suggestion that it could be the previous inhabitants did not go down well either, as some of their relatives still live on the Close and were at the meeting. I had to call the meeting firmly to order before fisticuffs broke out. We agreed not to cooperate with the press, but all are to remain vigilant, and any further information will be shared at a subsequent meeting.

There were two items of AOB (Any Other Business). Max brought up the question of a small white plastic picket fence erected by Ron and Bev in their front garden. He is convinced that this contravenes the contract we all signed for the freehold of our various residences. The general feeling of the meeting seemed to be that as the edifice in question is a mere six inches in height, it was not a problem, but Max was insistent. I don't mind reporting that I was not pleased. Poor Patsy looked extremely embarrassed by her husband's display of snobbery. As chairman, it is my duty to pour oil on troubled waters, so I volunteered to clarify the position later.

I then saw the opportunity to bring up the matter of

dog dirt. I was surprised that people were so reluctant to turn their attention to such an important and potentially hazardous issue. However, in the end we agreed to be extremely vigilant in the matter of dogs fouling the pavement. If things don't improve, we'll consider a petition to the relevant authorities. My campaign is coming on apace.

A rather gruesome sight greeted us as we left. Funeral directors were collecting the body from beneath the patio. The coffin was metal, painted a dull red. I felt myself shivering as it was loaded into the van.

1st February 1995

In the interests of fair play, I spent most of the day checking through the contracts for Brookside Close. Max proved to be right. When I told him, he was delighted. He couldn't wait to rush out and crow over his neighbour.

Unsurprisingly, Ron was not pleased. What he said was to the point: 'Maxie, have you ever stopped for one second to listen to yourself? There's all kinds of things being dug up over the road. Dead bodies and everything. Mandy Jordache is on the run somewhere, with them two kids. God only knows what's been gong on, but all you're worried about is some lousy little fence.'

Compared to finding an actual cadaver buried in a residential area, complaining about a small plastic erection does seem somewhat trivial. However, I had to take

Ron to task. All this speculation could become scaremongering in a trice.

In order to stem the flow of misinformation, I felt it my duty to liaise with the authorities. The residents' minds must be put at rest, and they do look to me for guidance on these occasions. I collared our local community policeman, PC Coburn, who has been in attendance. We have always got on well, so I thought he might be of assistance.

Unfortunately, our local boy in blue is kept as much in the dark about these matters as the community he polices. His special assignment is, as he put it, 'snack duty for the fat cats'. However, an interesting fact emerged. The investigation is being led by one Detective Inspector Coburn – brother to our chap. I asked if he could use his internal influence on his relation and he said he'd see what he could do.

Rumour has it that the body has been identified as Trevor Jordache, Mandy's errant husband. It is a disturbing possibility. The Jordaches came here originally to get away from him. At the time, number 10 was what they nowadays call a 'safe house', where women can take refuge from extremely violent men. Initially, Trevor was in prison for attacking his wife and putting her in hospital. A few months after Mandy, Beth and Rachel arrived, he found them. God knows how.

He was a thoroughly nasty piece of work. I remember a horrendous party they held once, for their wedding anniversary. Poor Mandy was obviously terrified. Trevor drank too much and constantly upbraided his wife with veiled threats if she put a toenail wrong. Jean and I scuttled away from that place as soon as we decently could. I blame myself. In my heart of hearts, I was certain there would be blows as soon as the door closed, but didn't know how to intervene.

Substance was added to the rumour by the fact that I was interviewed by DI Coburn this very afternoon. He went through how well I knew the Jordaches. I explained what sort of man Trevor Jordache was. His criminal record was common knowledge and I know for a fact that Mandy abhors violence in any form. I made it clear how impossible it is for her to be involved in murder.

'Nobody's accusing Mrs Jordache of anything at this point in time,' DI Coburn replied.

At this point in time. In other words, they're probably collecting sufficient evidence to make an arrest. My blood ran cold. DI Coburn is totally unlike our cheery neighbourhood PC. Perhaps his machine-like inhumanity is the reason he's a detective-inspector, while his younger sibling remains a constable.

He then asked me about a Thomas Sweeney, a.k.a. Sinbad, our window cleaner. What was his relationship to Mandy? When had it started? Even though I could see where this line of questioning was leading, I had to tell the truth. Yes, he and Mandy were involved before Trevor's funeral. Sinbad had been extremely helpful at the time, but that's just the sort of chap he is. It's in his nature. He'd do anything for anybody.

On that note, DI Coburn snapped his notebook shut

and got up to leave. He thanked me for my help and said I may need to make a fuller statement later. That's it for now. The interview was most unsatisfactory. I gave him as much information as I could, whilst he kept what he knew to himself.

The only hint I gleaned came as we parted.

'Good luck,' I said. 'Not that you'll need it.'

'No,' he replied with a look in his eye, 'I don't think we will.'

2nd February 1995

It's official. The body has been identified as one Trevor Jordache. Of course, we had to read about it in the newspapers. You would have thought after all our co-operation, the police would have let us or at least me, as the appointed community leader, know what was happening. Apparently, they're looking for Sinbad, Mandy and Beth. No doubt to 'help with their enquiries'.

The Close is virtually under siege. We've had the television people here and every local and national paper has its representative camped out in the street. None of us can leave our houses without having microphones and pencils shoved under our noses.

Not that they'll get any joy out of us. A conspiracy of silence has been jointly agreed by the residents of Brookside Close. The less we reveal, the less there will be to report. The less there is to report, the less reason they'll have for camping out on our doorsteps.

On a lighter note, the feud between Max and Casa Bevron is hotting up. Young Beverley has decided to 'go organic', as she puts it. I have to say it's the influence of my daughter. Patsy has always been most attentive to her and the children's health, but Bev is throwing herself into it with an enthusiasm that's almost bound to go awry.

I wish she'd sought my advice before she started. After all, I do have a measure of experience in these matters. Beverley has made the classic beginner's mistake at gardening. Realizing how essential it is to feed the soil, she ordered manure. It duly arrived – not in a neat little sack as she expected, but a full load from a farmer's truck, enough to satisfy the needs of the head gardener at Buck House. Sitting on the front lawn is a steaming pile somewhat taller than myself announcing its presence to anyone with a nose. Personally, I can't see what's wrong with the smell of Mother Nature, but needless to say, Max objects.

I've taken a bucketload of the stuff to feed to my roses. They'll be glad of it, although I can't say it's lessened the heap to any noticeable degree. I got the chance of a chat with Beverley and she reminded me of something rather disturbing.

A few months ago, Sinbad actually bought number 10, Brookside Close and became Mandy's landlord. As far as I know, he's not charging her much by way of rent. Sinbad said that the money came from his mother, who'd sold a house in Australia. At the time, nobody thought anything of it. We all knew he had a mother and that she'd emigrated to the Antipodes. Recent events, however, cast a quite different shadow over his story. As Bev suggested, there could have been insurance involved. I'm loathe to think so ill of my fellow citizens, but with every detail that's revealed, their actions seem a bit more suspicious. It brings to mind one of Jean's favourite films – *Double Indemnity*.

3rd February 1995

I couldn't believe my eyes when I opened my paper this morning. There on the front page was a picture of the Jordaches' rear garden. It could only have been taken from the living room of that traitor, Eddie Banks.

My God, I despair of humanity sometimes. He's let the weasels of the press crawl in behind the barbed wire. The whole sorry affair gets more sordid by the minute.

How could he let them in? I'm astonished that Rosie didn't put her foot down, if nothing else. I wonder what the price of betrayal is these days. What's the exchange rate for thirty pieces of silver?

I came across Mr Iscariot himself in the Close. I told him we'd all seen the fruits of his collusion. He had nothing to say for himself whatsoever. His only saving grace was that he looked extremely sheepish. No doubt the rest of the residents will make their opinions felt in due course.

Eddie Banks of all people. I still can't quite take it in.

He's normally the most upright of men, renowned for his activities on behalf of his fellow workers. How could he do such a thing? How could he let us all down?

I think I have solved the manure problem. Max was complaining bitterly about it, but Bev couldn't get anyone to remove it before the end of next week. It needed someone with a flair or organization to solve the problem. I have arranged to borrow the van from the florists on the Parade where Jean works. Commencing at dawn tomorrow, Beverley and I will bag the whole pile up, load it into the van and take it back whence it came. Max is to provide the bin bags. An operation worked out to exact military requirements.

4th February 1995

I should have had more faith. Eddie has returned to the fold once more. He shuffled up to me as Beverley and I were at work on the manure.

'About this photo lark,' he said. Not that 'lark' was an entirely appropriate phrase for what he did. 'I've given it a bit of thought and I can see you've got a point, so I want you to take this.'

He waved a piece of paper at me. It was a cheque for several hundred pounds, signed by the proprietor of one of Fleet Street's largest. I was quite taken aback. Eddie has authorized me to spend it as I see fit, so I shall make sure it goes to a good cause.

The poor lad looked thoroughly ashamed of himself. He wouldn't say precisely what brought about this change of heart, simply putting it down to seeing the error of his ways. I suspect Bev put her finger on it.

'Missis given you the bum's rush, has she?' was her comment.

Pure English it may not be. Accurate, I believe it is.

As if to offer a total contrast, Jimmy Corkhill turned up a short while later. I asked him whether he was visiting to gawp at proceedings across the way. The man didn't even have the decency to deny it.

'What if I have?' he said. 'Free country, isn't it?'

He then had the nerve to accuse Beverley and myself of 'loving every minute of it'. I do not understand how his twisted mind works. As it happened, he hadn't appeared merely to be a spectator. Oh no. He wants to get in on the act. Because the house used to belong to his brother and, even worse, because Sinbad is supposed to be his best friend, he has decided to sell his story to the highest bidder.

That bloodsucker doesn't know the meaning of honour. I pointed out to him that we, as residents, have agreed on a code of silence. Nobody is going to break it (apart from Eddie's temporary aberration). Corkhill was totally unperturbed.

As we were arguing, Cracker slipped her leash and headed straight for the police cordon. One has to admire the animal's sense of direction. She dashed straight under the ribbons with Corkhill in hot pursuit. The police prevented him from going in, but the dog evaded capture and disappeared round the side of the house into the garden itself.

Moments later, she emerged with a large bone in her mouth. Suddenly, the might of Fleet Street descended on dog and master. God knows what's been uncovered now. The police could scarcely get near the offending article for the throng of press parasites eagerly feeding on the latest titbit.

Disgusting as the spectacle was, there was nothing I could do. Corkhill stood there, posing and smirking, as flashguns went off and every journalist fired questions at him at once. I dread to think what tomorrow's headlines will bring.

5th February 1995

I might have known. The papers are full of some cock and bull rubbish about that flea-bitten mongrel of Corkhill's digging up possible further human remains. Utter poppycock. That infernal hound simply unearthed an old lamb bone it buried there last week. I don't know what can be done about that man. I wonder if it would be possible to take out an injunction.

I fear Beverley's in for a spot of bother. We took the manure back to the farm, but there was no-one around to take delivery. Eventually, I tracked down a lowly farm hand who told me where we could leave it. In the meantime, Bev was poking around some of the buildings. I advised her I didn't think she should be interfering, but that young woman has a mind of her own.

There were terrific squawks coming from one shack. Bev looked through a crack in the wall and her face turned white. The edifice was chock full of chickens. Being a kind-hearted soul, Beverley was immediately concerned.

'Did you see the state of the poor things?' she said. 'Stuck in those little boxes all day. You'd think someone would let them out for a fly around or something.'

I took a quick peek myself. They did look rather a sorry sight. As I remarked to Bev, I always prefer them stuffed, with a spot of gravy, myself. Besides, I don't actually think chickens can fly.

Never has my levity been worse timed. We got back to the van, with my companion practically in tears. I started the engine up, intending a speedy exit, when one of the chickens wandered right in front of our path. I dare say escape was pretty easy, the buildings looked distinctly derelict.

Before I could say a word of protest, Beverley had slipped her seat belt, scooped the bird up and jumped back into the front seat.

'Get going, before someone comes,' she cried.

The urgency in her voice was such that I'd driven the van out of the gates and half way down the main road before I had time to think.

I have colluded with a theft. Bev refuses to take the bird back. She's christened it Kiev and before we'd gone half a mile, it was obviously part of the family. What with her organic vegetables and fresh, free-range eggs,

Josh is going to be the healthiest child in Liverpool.

I didn't have the heart to tell her that Kiev is a cock.

I don't know how she managed to reconcile Ron to the keeping of livestock, but she did. All the neighbours were bidden to Casa Bevron this evening for a house-warming party. Jean got out of it by babysitting for our grandchildren, Thomas and Alice. I put in an appearance, flanked by the Farnhams.

Frankly, Bev has got Ron well under the thumb. The place has been completely redecorated in a distinctly feminine style. Everything that can be frilled has been. A little over the top for my taste, and beyond the pale as far as Max and Patsy are concerned, but each to their own. I suppose it's a classic example of what happens to a middle-aged man when he falls for a much younger woman. Let's just hope he can keep up with her. I must say, I enjoyed the buffet tremendously.

Conversation obviously centred around events at number 10. The possible scenarios got more and more far-fetched as the evening wore on. By the time I left, we had Sinbad worming his way into Mandy's good books, promising her the earth, on condition she gets rid of her husband. It all seems very far away from our well-meaning, stout and jovial window cleaner. But with Sinbad and the entire family still missing without explanation, even I am starting to fear the worst.

7th February 1995

The worst has happened. Mandy, Beth and Sinbad have been found and arrested. I was round at Patsy's when the news broke. It was the top item on the early morning round up. Even though we've been expecting something like this, it was a shock actually to hear it. There's an almost unreal quality to it all. Hearing Sinbad referred to as 'Thomas Sweeney' and the home of our neighbours as 'a suburban garden in Liverpool'. It's as though they're talking about a different place entirely, yet all this is happening under our very noses.

Apparently, they've been on the run in Ireland for the whole week. The police took them to Dublin headquarters last night and shipped them back to England this morning. They are now in the custody of Merseyside police officers. In other words, they've been left to the tender mercies of Detective Inspector Coburn.

It was also reported that young Rachel was with them at the time. She's only fifteen. Who's going to take care of her? I dread to think of what that poor girl's going through. What they all are.

The ranks of the press have swelled. Cars and vans have been turning up all day. The litter and noise is appalling. However, I dare not go near them to protest. I'd simply get bombarded with questions for my pains. These wretches don't care how much they intrude on people's lives, nor how much inconvenience they cause.

One titbit emerged. It has been confirmed that the

bone Corkhill's mutt found indeed belonged to someone's Sunday joint. Just as I suspected. I'd like to know how much they paid him for that cock and bull story of his. They've virtually made him out to be some kind of local hero. I thoroughly object to him making money out of that wretched creature. It's immoral.

As I left Patsy's, I was collared by Beverley. More trouble. Ron has put his foot down. Kiev has to go. I thought his indulgence was too good to last. Would I give her a lift back to the farm? Before I had a chance to get a word in edgeways, Max was making the arrangements on my behalf. He and that cockerel have not seen eye to eye. Max is something of a night owl and did not take kindly to being woken up literally at cock crow.

Bev also mentioned that she's enrolling young Josh in a nursery – the same one Patricia's applied to for my granddaughter Alice. Max was less than delighted.

'Do you ever get the feeling that the neighbours are trying to invade our lives?' he commented when Bev had gone back inside.

Personally, I think community spirit is an excellent thing. Patricia may be glad of some support at the nursery. She's chosen it because of its liberal attitudes, but Alice still might not be accepted. Babies with Down's Syndrome are so often seen as nothing but problems by people who are unwilling to try to understand them.

I drove Ben back down to the farm, with her keeping Kiev tucked under her jacket. We crept in at the front gate and as before, there was no-one around. I wanted to simply leave the bird in the middle of the yard where we'd found it, but Bev insisted on finding some shelter. There was a mild drizzle and she didn't want her former pet to catch cold.

There were three or four long, low shed-type affairs. Bev peeked into one as before and came away looking most distressed. I could see I was in for a hard time persuading her to put Kiev back where he belonged.

We prowled around the back of the buildings to see if there was a less crowded spot for him. We came across a corner where one of the planks had broken loose. No doubt that's how Kiev initially made his escape. As we watched, four chickens fluttered out.

'I can't do it,' Bev sobbed. 'I can't just leave Kiev here. And what about his mates? It's no use, I've got to rescue them.'

The upshot was that far from getting rid of one bird, we travelled back with an extra four. At least, the new ones are genuine chickens. Bev has christened them Nugget, Butty, Ham Pie and Fried Rice. Presumably in honour of their narrow escape.

Jean thinks the whole affair is highly amusing. She says I've got a soft spot for Bev and that she can wrap me round her little finger. But Jean has always eyed with suspicion my extremely innocent friendship with the younger elements of the fairer sex. I like women. That's all. Nothing sordid in that, is there? But Jean always implies that there are other motives. I mean, how could I with my morals and respect for Jean? Well, there was that one occasion many years ago with young Patsy's nanny, and then that unfortunate misunderstanding with the maid when we lived in Spain. But I assure you, they were merely temporary aberrations.

8th February 1995

Rosie Banks came over this morning. It seems she has offered to look after Rachel Jordache while her mother and sister are being held in custody. She and Eddie managed to sneak her in by the sensible expedient of not making a fuss. They simply drove out with their younger son, Lee, who's Rachel's great friend, and drove back with an extra child in tow. It proves that not talking to the press works. If anyone had leaked the connection, the Banks would have been besieged.

Of course, it wasn't long before the vultures realized there was fresh meat, but at least Rachel was indoors by then. Rosie told me she's been very quiet, not eating and not saying a word about what happened in Ireland. Not unnaturally, the Banks are worried about how to handle her and how long the situation is likely to continue. I had very little to offer them by way of comfort.

The throng of reporters and ghoulish sightseers is growing by the minute. Under the circumstances, I thought it best to call another meeting of the B.R.A. Jean made an impressive spread for us and nearly everyone attended. Apologies were accepted from Rosie and Eddie Banks.

One most welcome member was Barry Grant, owner of number 5 and Max's business partner in Grants

Restaurant. He is also proprietor of the local night spot, La Luz, and employs one James Corkhill as general factotum. His business methods are somewhat dubious, but if anyone can handle Corkhill, he can.

Barry's solution was that we should simply 'blank' the press. As Patricia commented, that's easier said than done. Especially with quisling Corkhill betraying everything he knows to the enemy. The meeting detailed Barry to convey our views forcefully to his employee.

In Ron's opinion, we should tell the press anything that comes into our heads, as long as it is *not* true, in order to relieve them of some of their ill-gotten gains. The money thus raised could go towards a fund for the Jordaches. In a novel way, the idea is attractive, but even some innocent remark could worsen poor Mrs Jordache's plight. I feel the best thing to do is to avoid any contact whatsoever.

I proposed that we form a sub-committee of the B.R.A. to handle all cases of press intrusion on an ad hoc basis. This sub-committee, consisting of two people, plus myself, could intervene and do what they can to solve matters. It would then report back to the regular residents' meetings.

I regret to say this suggestion landed on distinctly stony ground. When I asked for nominations, not a single hand was raised. Not one person was prepared to spare the time for this vital task. I was most disappointed. Max and Barry have the restaurant. Ron's running two shops and so on and so forth. Even Patricia failed to back me up, although I'd hardly expect her to be able to contribute. Thomas and young Alice are quite enough for one person to cope with.

The net result was that I volunteered to perform the duties of sole sub-committee member. This motion was carried unanimously.

After that, the meeting degenerated into a rather heated discussion about animal rights. Beverley has insisted that her household becomes vegetarian. Ron, however, is not keen. Before the meeting started, he slipped into the kitchen and laid hands on a ham sandwich. He was just about to take a bite, when Ben came in. Caught in the act, by God! She snatched the offending foodstuff from his lips and ushered him firmly into the living room. Under her beady eye, he was allowed nothing but salad.

Under A.O.B., Max asked for a ruling on keeping livestock in a residential area. His point is that he has two children playing next door and doesn't want them exposed to all kinds of disease. He asked Ron to intervene. Quite unfairly, in my opinion. The poor man was positively slavering for a slice of chicken, but didn't dare go against the wishes of his good lady. In the end, I left it to the two parties concerned to sort out.

The whole thing is ridiculously trivial. Their predicament pales into insignificance when compared to the situation facing Mandy and Sinbad.

9th February 1995

My duties as sole press sub-committee member could prove difficult. As soon as Ron set foot outside his house this morning, he was set upon by a gang of ghouls. He barely got away to open up the Trading Post. Mind you, he's making a huge profit out of all this. I saw him take delivery of hundreds of boxes of chocolate bars, crisps and the like. Sightseers and press alike are certainly adding to Ron's coffers.

The Jordache case is still item number one on the television. Rosie came over for a bit of a heart-to-heart. She said she'd found Rachel sitting disconsolately on the bed, listening to the radio speculating about what's to happen to her mother and sister. Since she got to the Banks's, she's scarcely eaten a meal. On the one hand, hearing the rubbish that's reported can only upset her. On the other, it's impossible to get proper information from any other source. The poor girl is going out of her mind with worry, not knowing what's going on.

One item of news that was reported accurately was the disclosure of Jimmy Corkhill's true character. The so-called local hero turns out to be a known burglar with a criminal record. Of course, the tone adopted by the papers was one of shock and outrage, as if it wasn't they who'd praised him to the skies in the first place.

Corkhill stormed round to the Close, seething with self-righteousness. I wasn't in, but Patricia spoke to him. He'd got it into his head that it was I who had leaked his sordid details to the press. She pointed out to him that only last night, I had insisted on a motion to ignore the press, so it was extremely unlikely that I would crack. His past is scarcely secret. No doubt his various court cases were recorded in the very papers he's complaining about now. Perhaps this will shut him up. Patricia said his indignation was hilarious.

Just as well she had something to laugh at. Taking young Alice to the nursery proved a major disappointment. They wouldn't take her. They said they haven't got the staff or the facilities to look after a baby with Downs. It might create difficulties with the other children. Basically, it doesn't suit their trendy image.

I can't remember the last time I saw Patricia so angry and upset. The place advertises itself as being anti-discrimination, but apparently this doesn't include disabled children.

Max was just as hurt. He was all for storming the place and insisting they take Alice. Patricia managed to calm him down. It's not fair to use a baby as some sort of a weapon. I feel so very deeply for both of them, but there's nothing Jean and I can do, except hold their hands and listen.

11th February 1995

I met up with Rosie on the Parade this afternoon. She looks worn out. The press hounding goes on and on. The entire family's feeling the strain. Not only can Rachel not leave the house without being set on, she can't even go to the window. A mere glance out of her bedroom earlier today brought photographers trampling through the flower beds, staring and snapping.

The situation's abominable. School is totally out of the question. The head teacher told Rosie it would be better for Rachel to stay off until things have cooled down. It's depressing for her, but the only solution. If she tried to get out, she'd be followed and not allowed a minute's peace.

Rosie's really worried about Rachel's state of mind, however. She broke down in tears, anxious that she will be put in a home and that Mandy and Beth will be locked up forever. Rosie did her best to comfort her. The woman is a true Christian. She reassured Rachel she was welcome in their home for as long as it takes and mentioned her confidence that the prisoners will be released soon.

Then Rachel dropped a bombshell. She was absolutely adamant that Mandy and Beth will be incarcerated for good.

'They'll never let them go for what they did,' she said. 'It was murder. Mum and our Beth killed my Dad. I know it's true, because they told me.'

Could it be right? Could mild-mannered Mrs Jordache have brought herself to commit such a heinous crime? And Beth? A young girl, still in her teens? A medical student about to dedicate her life to saving others? It's unbelievable.

On the other hand, Rachel wouldn't lie about something like this.

If only we knew the truth.

One thing's for sure – Sinbad is thankfully out of the frame. He was released without charge this afternoon. Barry Grant has offered him a bed, as number 10 is still sealed. Jimmy Corkhill managed to sneak him in to number 5 under the cover of darkness. So far, the press aren't aware of his presence on the close. I'm surprised our friend Corkhill isn't selling tickets.

12th February 1995

I caught Corkhill red-handed this afternoon. His wretched hound was doing its business once again right under the sign forbidding it to do so. Some sixth sense told me what was going on, so I rushed out, pooper scooper in hand to bring the miscreant to justice.

Corkhill has the nerve to claim the pile was an accident. Accident? He positively encouraged it. It's utterly abhorrent. A hazard to public health. I shall see about getting him prosecuted for this.

I handed him the pooper scooper and insisted he remove the offending item. We'll never know if he would have done so, as Ron and Bev were also lying in wait behind the net curtains, waiting for Public Enemy Number 1 to put in an appearance. It seems the four chickens have been slaughtered. Their dreams of fresh eggs for the youngster have been dashed. Only Kiev the cockerel is left. The culprit appears to be canine.

Corkhill denied everything, of course, and referred to

his long-suffering wife, Jackie, for an alibi. No doubt Ron will be checking up in due course.

In the midst of the row, Barry Grant showed up, looking less than pleased. Faced with such heavy opposition, Corkhill beat a hasty retreat – with my pooper scooper in his hand! Has the man no moral fibre?

13th February 1995

Events become more disturbing by the day. Mrs Jordache has been charged with the murder of her husband and Beth with conspiracy to murder. Against all odds, they've been granted bail. I thought it wouldn't have been possible with such serious charges against them, but a combination of prosecution incompetency and previous good character won the day.

Of course, it's ludicrous to keep those two women behind bars. Even if it is proved that they did murder Trevor, it was sure to have been in self-defence. Everyone knew the man was a monster. They're hardly likely to go on a killing spree.

They're holed up at Barry Grant's with Sinbad until their house is opened up by the police. It can't be much fun for them, cowering in the dark with the curtains drawn against the parasites of the press.

I might have known Corkhill wouldn't keep his big mouth shut for long. I found Sinbad hovering in the bushes outside my house, desperate for a word. He thrust this morning's paper into my hand. The headline was unbelievable - HOUSE OF HORRORS GANGLAND SECRET.

The blurb went on to describe number 10, Brookside Close as a safe house for some of England's most notorious gangsters. Meaning that rogue Corkhill and his clan. According to the ignoble fourth estate, the place was the hideout for 'a gang of hard men as feared and notorious as the Sicilian mafiosi, where they planned one criminal caper after another'.

The man's a rank outsider, selling his soul to these charlatans. As if the good name of Brookside Close hasn't suffered enough already at the hands of these hacks.

Ron invited me in for a coffee later on. He too was furious at the headlines. Worse than that, he was about ready to give up. He actually spoke of selling up and moving. I had to give him a good talking to. Was he really going to let the likes of Corkhill drive him away? An Englishman's home is his castle. Now's the time to stand up and be counted. Repel these intruders, be they chicken rustlers or ferrets from Fleet Street. Bev was behind me all the way and together we put the fighting spirit back into our noble shopkeeper.

In fact, Ron was so inspired, he decided to spend tonight in his shed, waiting for whatever – or possibly, whoever – is behind the chicken slaughter.

14th February 1995

How do I get myself into these things?

Last night, Jean had a fancy for one of Mick Johnson's excellent Hawaiian pizzas – ham and pineapple, with extra cheese. With all her interest in the alternative lifestyle, I'm very glad she shows no sign of becoming a vegetarian. Although, I must say I don't care for pizza myself – doesn't seem like real food. As I emerged from the Pizza Parlour with supper under my arm, who should I bump into than Corkhill himself, large as life. He and Cracker were waltzing down the Parade without a care in the world.

The very sight of him made my blood boil. I immediately began to remonstrate with him about his deplorable misconduct of late. Not content with using Brookside Close as a public convenience for his dog, he seems determined to drag its reputation through the mire as well. As Chairman of the B.R.A., it was clearly my duty to let him know in no uncertain terms that the residents will *not* stand for it. I intend to pursue every avenue open to me to run him out of the Close for good.

Corkhill's response was typically laconic. Called me 'Grandad' and refused to take any responsibility whatsoever for his actions.

If I couldn't get through to him, there are those who can. As we were speaking, a police car drew up and DI Coburn got out. He said he was looking for a Mr Jimmy Corkhill. I was only too happy to point out said gentleman. DI Coburn then proceeded to invite Corkhill to accompany him to the police station, where he was wanted for questioning about his time in residence at 10 Brookside Close. The House Of Hell, as the tabloids put it.

Retribution and Nemesis were at hand. Immediately, Corkhill started to bluster, claiming that the papers had blown everything out of proportion. The truth will out when the wretch is in trouble. DI Coburn was unmoved by his pleadings. Corkhill was pushed into the car, whingeing and whining and bumping his head.

A problem emerged. What to do about Cracker the dog. A prison cell was hardly an appropriate kennel. Before I could say a word, Corkhill thrust her lead into my hand. I objected that for me to look after her was quite out of the question, but DI Coburn pointed out that I would be helping the police with their work. After that, how could I refuse?

The car drove off and I was left with man's best friend.

Jean was less than overjoyed to meet our new house guest. Especially since the episode had meant her pizza had got cold. Still, like the trooper she is, she foraged in the fridge for something to feed the dog. There was a substantial piece of cold chicken waiting to be turned into sandwiches. Wonder of wonders, Cracker could not be induced to touch it.

That set me thinking. Ron Dixon was convinced that his chicken rustler was a canine and that the most likely suspect was my new-found four-legged friend. However, Cracker's taste in meat proved that she could not have been the culprit.

Away from her master, she really is quite a companion, wagging her tail and obviously appreciative of all Jean and I were trying to do for her. It occurred to me that I could take advantage of Corkhill's arrest to teach her some lavatorial etiquette. By the time her errant master returns, I hope to have instilled some discipline into her.

Jean popped some sausages under the grill, while I went round to Ron's to tell him to eliminate Cracker from his enquiries. I found him in his shed, wrapped up in a totally inadequate blanket with only a thermos flask for company. I fear the man had a most uncomfortable and fruitless vigil.

15th February 1995

I could get used to having a dog around the place. Jean and I left her in the kitchen to sleep, but the poor old girl was obviously lonely. We could hear her pathetic whining from the bedroom. No doubt she was missing her master - not that he deserves such devotion. In the end, I had to let her sleep on the bed. Jean decamped to the spare room, as she declared there wasn't enough room for the three of us.

I was awakened by a doggy tongue giving my face a wash. Somehow, Cracker had managed to work her way under the covers. We got up together and went for a nice long walk. She's no trouble at all to train. Every fault of hers can be laid at Corkhill's door. I shall miss her when she's reclaimed.

It seems it wasn't only chicken rustlers creeping around under the cover of darkness. The Jordaches moved back into number 10 yesterday evening. The hacks are not much in evidence at night, even though they're a bunch of vampires. Presumably, they spend their evenings getting thoroughly inebriated at their papers' expense.

The rags managed to glean a story nonetheless. Again, there's been a leak, this time about young Beth's background. Again, the headlines screamed. BODY IN GARDEN: GIRL IN GAY SEX STORM and GAY LOVE SECRET OF MURDER SUSPECT. To be fair, one of the problems I've always had with Beth is how little she kept her deviant sexuality under wraps. It's hardly a secret that she's a lesbian. I suppose it wouldn't have made such a good headline if the tabloids couldn't suggest that they were 'revealing' something.

In the interest of justice, however, such stuff should not be allowed to be printed. The implication is clearly that Beth and her mother are two man-hating viragos, who murdered an innocent man. No mention is made of his utter brutality. It's trial by press. How are they going to get a fair trial, when every juror will have been influenced by what they've read and seen?

Jean was most upset to read about it. She and I have agreed to differ in our views about Beth Jordache's sexual preference. In fact, it is not a subject we can discuss easily, since Jean once revealed that she too had a female lover when she was young. Even though it was before she met me, the thought of it still hurts. Thank

God it happened in less 'trendy' days and it thankfully came to nothing but confused feelings. It quite turns my stomach at the very memory.

I remember when I first found out, I couldn't bear to go near my beloved wife. It took weeks for me to recover my equilibrium. It was certainly a factor in my regrettable dalliance with arch-harpy, Audrey Manners. I have also been thinking that it could put into some kind of perspective my natural 'wanderlust'. These latest, lefty social worker types could make some kind of connection, I'm sure.

I slipped over to number 10 this afternoon to have a quiet word. Unsurprisingly, the atmosphere in the house is distinctly gloomy. Rachel won't speak to her mother and none of them dares leave the house. There wasn't much I could say, except to offer my support, both as Chairman of the B.R.A. and as a neighbour. I fear there are very dark days ahead.

19th February 1995

Just as I got used to having Cracker around, she was snatched from my arms. Corkhill got back the day before yesterday. The police released him without charge – unfortunately. Apparently, they gave him a nasty scare over his lies to the press, but they knew all along there wasn't a word of truth in any of the articles. Even they knew it was obvious he was incapable of any crime involving brains.

Dog and master trotted off happily. The last I saw of my pal was her pulling at the lead in order to relieve herself in the gutter. My training, at least, has paid off.

The man really isn't fit to take care of a fine animal like Cracker. Every morning since his return, Cracker has found a way to my back door. She's a dashed intelligent creature – knows full well that Jean is less than approving of her continued presence. The little devil puts in an appearance as soon as Jean is out of the way. We have secret sausage feasts together. If it weren't for the fact that I don't want to arouse any sibling rivalry, I'd seriously consider getting a dog of my own.

21st February 1995

Excellent news arrived in the post this morning. I have been chosen as area delegate for the National Conference of Residents' Associations in Brighton. I leave at the end of the week, which will give me very little time to canvas everyone's views. If I'm to represent the good citizens of this community, it's vital I know what issues are important to them. I want to be the voice of the man in the street.

I also had an excellent idea. Good old Ted Bond has retired to Hove, just down the road from where the conference is to be held. It occurred to me that Jean and I could look him up whilst we're in the area. It might make quite a pleasant break of it. Jean has always enjoyed going down to Brighton. With my expenses covered by B.R.A. funds, the trip shouldn't break the bank either.

Jean had already left by the time I'd got up and opened the post. There was a cookery demonstration at the over-fifties club. (Given, I might add, by Mick Johnson, a dab hand at considerably more than a pizza.) I found her knee deep in rump steak and cooking oil.

I couldn't persuade Jean to come to the conference with me. She said she didn't relish being my secretary for a week, then listening to me and Ted Bond swapping endless stories about National Service. I was disappointed, but once Jean has made up her mind about something, there's no earthly point in arguing.

There was only one fly in the ointment – Audrey Manners. She was at the club and overheard my discussion with Jean re attendance at the conference. As soon as she heard Jean refuse to go, she wanted to take her place. Naturally, I declined. That woman is the bane of my life. One tiny slip and I'm left with a never-ending problem.

I keep going over and over our one night of sordid dalliance. I would do anything to change things. I shouldn't blame Jean. The shock of finding out about her and her lady 'friends' adversely affected the old equipment. Jean was terribly decent about it. It's my own stupid, idiotic fault. That sort of failure does terrible things to a man. I felt as if I was only half a person. As if I was failing Jean in the most basic way.

Audrey was overwhelmingly persistent. She was all over me, saying I would never find out if it was something wrong with me. Then there was that terrible evening when I gave in to her siren's song and my own wretched weakness. I realized, even as our legs were loathsomely entwined, that I was betraying the woman I love. The only redeeming factor being that Audrey seemed to cure me of my 'problem'.

I shudder with remorse every time I remember. How can I live with myself after what I've done? Forty years of trust gone in an instant. There's nothing I can do. I can't talk to anyone about it. If I told Jean, she'd leave me. That's my one fear. I don't deserve a woman like her in any case. How could I have been so reckless?

To cap it all, the Manners woman has wheedled her way into Jean's good graces. She will insist on calling me 'Major'. To my eternal shame, I embellished a little about my status when I first met Audrey. It was a ridiculous attempt at self-importance. Jean finds the whole thing amusing. The poor woman has such touching faith in me, she would never dream there was anything between us.

The worst thing about this 'Major' business is that it is a constant reminder of the truth about my father. I pray to God that Patricia, Max and my loyal friends never find out the truth about his supposedly heroic military career.

22nd February 1995

The Jordaches are slowly emerging back into society. I

met Mandy Jordache in the Trading Post. The atmosphere as she came in was appalling. The temperature dropped by several degrees. What do you say to someone on a murder charge? The silence was deafening.

She asked for twenty Benson & Hedges, although Ron told me afterwards he'd never known her buy cigarettes before. No doubt it's the strain telling. I felt for the poor woman. I've never seen anyone look quite so withdrawn and haggard. Her face was as grey as the wall of a prison cell.

It's a pity Beth can't learn some of her mother's self-effacement. Apparently, she took offence at the way another customer was whispering about her and slammed a bag of flour on to the counter so hard it burst. Counter, goods and shopkeeper were covered in the stuff. I've never seen Ron Dixon look so pale.

A most mysterious incident occurred later. Yesterday, Jean told me Audrey's long-lost brother had shown up at the cookery demonstration. I gather Jean was rather taken with him. When I popped into the flower-shop to see her, she was with a seedy-looking gent, whom she introduced as George Manners. I complimented him on his resemblance to Audrey, saying it was easy to see he was her elder brother.

At this, the man looked astounded. It turns out he's her husband, who's spent the past few years in Kenya. He and Audrey were merely separated, not even divorced. We had been under the impression that he'd passed away. Audrey has always represented herself as a widow. It looks like reports of his death were much exaggerated.

15th March 1995

The conference was superb. One of the most enlightening trips I've had in years. My week with Tom was a feast of good malt whiskey and nostalgia.

However, there have been the most tremendous happenings whilst I've been away. Jean and I had a long debriefing session. For a start, she's been conned out of some three hundred pounds. It seems that Audrey's miraculous spouse sold timeshares for a living and Jean fell for his patter. I must say I was surprised at her naivety. It was obvious to all and sundry that the man was a charlatan.

But there was far worse to come. No sooner had Jean signed on the fraudulent dotted line, than George Manners collapsed in our front garden. Jean called an ambulance, but he was dead on arrival. This all happened yesterday afternoon. Unfortunately, she couldn't get hold of me, or I'd have been back here twelve hours sooner.

It seems he died of some mysterious virus, no doubt the result of his foreign travel. Although even when I met him, he didn't strike me as being overly healthy. Audrey is not only distraught, but unwell to boot. She's coughing her heart out in the spare room even as I write. I couldn't help wondering if there wasn't something a tad convenient about her illness, until she made an appearance, white as a sheet, and fainted in the hallway.

Another tragedy has hit the Close. Mick Johnson was looking after a young lad, Gary Salter, as a sort of unofficial foster parent. The man has a heart of gold. Gary had been something of a tearaway, but Mick worked wonders. The result was that the lad found himself a job at the local leisure centre. On his very first day, whilst acting as a lifeguard, he fell into the pool and died instantly. Yet it appears he didn't drown and no-one is sure of the precise cause of death.

It's extremely disturbing. Patricia is worried because Thomas is running a temperature and vomiting. The eldest Banks boy, Carl, is on the sick list. There must be a connection. People are dropping like flies. You can't tell me this is some grand coincidence.

My anxieties are shared by Mick Johnson. He came round to ask me if I'd heard anything more about the virus that killed George Manners. It's his belief that George and Gary succumbed to the same illness. I'm inclined to agree.

We called the doctor in to have a look at Audrey. He wasn't sure what was wrong with her, but said it could possibly be a mild version of the bug that attacked her deceased husband. She refused to go into hospital, as she didn't want to make a fuss. Frankly, it would be far less inconvenient for us if she did go in.

Jean is not taking the situation seriously. As far as she's concerned, there's simply a nasty flu bug going around, of the type you get every winter on every street in Great Britain. She's completely disregarding young Gary's demise and that of George Manners. Not to mention the fact that our grandson is ill, as is Carl Banks and now Audrey. She scoffed at the idea of warning the other residents of a possible epidemic, accusing me of scaremongering. I disagree and will be disseminating information at the earliest opportunity. Unlike Jean, I have never found Nero a particularly inspiring role model.

16th March 1995

First thing this morning, I was at Max and Patricia's to tell them I have reason to believe the so-called bug Thomas has picked up may be the deadly virus that accounted for George Manners. I advised them in no uncertain terms to have him checked by a specialist at the hospital straight away.

My words fell on deaf ears. To be fair, Thomas was a hell of a lot brighter. Our little soldier was tucked up on the sofa, eating a solid breakfast and looking like his old self. I still think they should take him to the GP at least.

I regret to report that Patricia and Max treated my concerns with considerable levity. They seem to find my grandson's health the source of crass humour, implying I was simply trying to whip up a bit of hysteria, whilst succumbing to a number of conspiracy theories.

They were far more interested in Max's latest business trip. He's being sent to Florida to look into some of Barry Grant's affairs. I'm not entirely happy about him being whisked off at the whim of his partner. He should be here with his family in this time of impending crisis. However, I can see the attractions of a free trip to Florida weigh heavily.

Eddie Banks was no better. I popped in to see how his son Carl was doing. Again, he's much improved, although not yet in perfect health. Indeed, Eddie feels his son is starting to milk his illness to get Rosie chasing round after him.

17th March 1995

Why won't anyone listen to me and Mick? We have an epidemic on our hands for which we are totally unprepared. I've been scouring my medical dictionaries trying to track down this blasted virus, with no luck whatsoever. The combination of symptoms – fever, sore throat, vomiting, all of which come and go – is nowhere to be found.

Jean tried to persuade me to give it up. I realize amateur diagnoses can do more harm than good, but I've got to do something. She herself is not exactly on top form. I hope to God it's merely exhaustion. She's been running herself ragged looking after Audrey. I strongly suspect she's feverish, but the most she'll confess to is a feeling of light-headedness, brought on by a lack of breakfast.

Audrey hasn't improved and needs a lot of care. It isn't good for Jean. I know I ought to shoulder more of the burden, but I can't bear to be in the same room as the woman. Particularly not alone. The appropriate place for her is in hospital, whither she adamantly refuses to go. In a sickly-sweet, ridiculously self-effacing way, she is as stubborn as a mule. So we're stuck with her for the duration.

Thomas is going downhill too. Patsy takes after her mother in having a rather too robust attitude to health. He's been vomiting again and I'm worried about him becoming dehydrated. Patricia's doing all the right things, except getting the medics in. Max went off America-bound this morning leaving her to cope with the two children on her own. I fear the worst.

18th March 1995

There's no doubt about it. This virus is extremely serious and extremely infectious. Mick Johnson was summoned to see a pathologist at the hospital yesterday. It turns out we were right. The official word is that the virus that killed George Manners was also responsible for young Gary's sad demise. Any one of us could have it.

I met Mick in the Close. He had just been trying to persuade Patricia to get Thomas checked, despite his apparent recovery. As we were lamenting the scepticism we've met at every turn, Patsy came running out. She was as white as a sheet. Thomas had suddenly started vomiting blood.

I dashed in to help. While I cuddled my grandson, Patricia phoned for an ambulance. The poor lad had coughed up a hell of a lot of blood and his temperature was going through the roof. Naturally, he was absolutely terrified. I tried to comfort him, telling him everything was going to be fine, but it was a tremendous effort. My stomach felt like lead. It was all I could do to keep my hands from shaking visibly. Thomas is seriously ill.

Patricia went with him in the ambulance, while I went to check on my own pair of invalids. I got the shock of my life when I stepped through the door. The first thing I saw was a broken cup in the hall. I bent to pick it up, before I realized Jean was unconscious on the kitchen floor.

By the time I'd got her into bed, she had woken up a bit. Whatever this infection is, its symptoms come and go with alarming rapidity. Jean said she was literally overcome in seconds. Didn't even get the chance to reach a chair. I made her promise not to stir. She must have got a fright, because she didn't even put up an argument.

Audrey's much the same. I had to tell her that Jean wasn't well, if only because I shall be taking over as carer. Of course, I tried to make light of it. Didn't mention the collapse and reduced Jean's temperature by several degrees. Much as I dislike her, I don't want to make Audrey more anxious than I need when she's so ill herself. Even so, there was no disguising the fact that Jean is confined to bed and therefore in a pretty bad way.

19th March 1995

Audrey took a turn for the worse in the night. I was at my wits' end. She's been feverish for so many days, she's becoming dangerously dehydrated. Yet, she still wouldn't let me send for an ambulance. Said she wouldn't dream of calling them out in the middle of the night. By this morning, she was barely conscious. I took it upon myself to get her into hospital. The doctor said she should have been there days ago.

I'll never forgive myself. Her condition is critical. If only I'd persuaded her to go sooner. If only she'd listened. If only she didn't have this ridiculous crush on me. I know I didn't try as hard as I could have done, because it worried me that I was just trying to get rid of her. My wretched over-emotionalism may have been fatal.

Jean ought to go into hospital as well. I'm quite clear about that – no question whatever. It's perfectly obvious that she's going the same way as Audrey. Yet when the ambulance for Audrey arrived, there was Jean clinging on to the front-door frame for support, insisting on saying goodbye.

Whenever I remonstrate about her refusal to see sense, she accuses me of fussing and insists she's just got a touch of flu. Flu! Who on earth does she think she's kidding?

Quite apart from anything else, she should be convinced by the attitude of the authorities. Environmental health officers descended on the Close, complete with protective clothing, to inspect the drains. The pizza parlour's been closed down and samples have been taken from Ron's perishables at the Trading Post. They are obviously taking the situation seriously, why can't Jean?

The sufferers are all getting worse. I met Eddie on his way to work and he told me Carl has had a relapse. Patricia is in a terrible state. Thomas has been put in an isolation ward. She spent the entire day there, leaning on the glass, unable to get any closer to her son. They've put him on a drip and various monitors, so he's lying there alone, a mass of tubes. Alice has been taken in too for observation. At least, Patsy can visit her properly and give her a cuddle.

I desperately want to be with them, but I daren't leave Jean alone. This wretched virus brings reversals so suddenly, I cannot allow her to be by herself for more than a very few minutes at the most.

21st March 1995

Jean is much better this morning, thank God. She's up and about and even eating. It's quite remarkable. Her symptoms were identical to Audrey's, yet she genuinely appears to be on the road to recovery.

I tucked Jean up on the sofa and took the opportunity to pop round to Patsy's. I found her very depressed and low. Thomas is still unconscious. She'd only come back for a bath and a change of clothes, before going back to the hospital.

'He's lying there in that room all on his own,' she said. 'I just want to be with him. I just want to hold him.'

I didn't know what to say. One feels so damned inadequate at times like these. All I could do was to be as positive as I could. Thomas is a fighter. Tough as old boots, like his grandmother. He'll pull through, I told Patsy. Besides, he has youth and general good health on his side. He was as fit as a fiddle before this virus attacked him.

While I was making us both a nice strong cup of coffee, we got a visit from Barry Grant's girlfriend, Emma. He's disappeared, leaving her in a state of distress. Patricia offered practical comfort by reminding her that Barry's probably gone to Florida with Max. Personally, I feel Mr Grant has disappeared in fear of this impending virus. Incidentally, Max appears to have gone AWOL. Patsy's been trying to get through to him without success. Let's hope he makes contact soon. She needs him by her side at a time like this.

A few minutes later, we had another visitor, Dr Horton from the General came round looking for yours truly. He wanted me to arrange a special B.R.A. meeting. At first I was none too keen. What with Jean, Thomas and Patsy, not to mention Audrey, I had my own family to think about. But Dr Horton was insistent. He said he needed this meeting urgently.

Luckily, young Emma stepped into the breach. The meeting will be held tomorrow chez Barry Grant. As he's vanished, she's been left in charge of his house. She also volunteered to round everyone up. It was a great relief, although Dr Horton's parting words put the fear of God into me.

'I can't emphasize strongly enough how important this meeting is,' he said darkly. 'For everybody.'

22nd March 1995

In all my years as a pharmacist, I've never come across anything like this. It's like lassa fever or something. Even in England, such things are not unknown. With modern travel, infections can move from country to country very easily.

I telephoned the hospital to see how Audrey was doing. No better. Max is still incommunicado. Patsy's getting quite desperate. She's keeping a vigil by the lad's bedside, but needs her husband by her side.

Jean wasn't looking too bright this morning. Her colour's poor and I suspect her temperature's gone up again. Although she insisted I went to the residents' association meeting, I was most reluctant to leave her. The others were counting on their chairman's support, she said. I saw her point. As a retired chemist I've got to use whatever expertise I have to beat this blasted bug before it claims another victim.

As I was about to leave, I received a call from Dr Horton. He'd been delayed at the hospital and wanted me to break the bad news. It seems the medical authorities now have evidence that all the illnesses and deaths could be linked. They may be the result of some highly contagious virus. Precisely what Mick Johnson and I have been saying all along.

I must say I'm glad I put my personal feelings aside to attend the meeting. As soon as I'd told everyone the situation, there was panic and rumour. Killer virus. We're all going to die of AIDS. That sort of thing. Then everybody started accusing everyone else of being the cause. Mick's pizzas, Ron's perishables or Beverley's chickens. I managed to calm things down by the time Dr Horton arrived.

His report was grave. We have an official epidemic on our hands. The cause is unknown. It's unlikely to be a zynotic strain, which means it can't be passed from animals to humans, so Kiev is in the clear. Apart from that, they know nothing.

Dr Horton proposed that the immediate area be cordoned off. Health checks for everyone will be arranged on site and a mobile clinic will be stationed at the edge of the Close.

Given the amount of hysteria expressed at the meeting, I was astonished to find that not everyone was willing to co-operate. In particular, Ron and Beverley insisted they were off to stay with relatives. We were still arguing about it as we left. I confess I was shocked by their lack of team spirit. We've got to stick together. There's no question of simply carrying on as normal.

Suddenly, I heard my name called urgently. Corkhill came running up with Cracker.

'Bing. Quick,' he panted. 'It's your Jean. I think she's dead.'

Dr Horton and I dashed back, to find Jean unconscious once again. Thanks to the good doctor's ministrations, she was soon back in bed and comfortable. It seems that Cracker slipped her lead and went on the prowl for sausages. Corkhill gave chase and spotted

Jean through the french windows. I never thought I'd have reason to thank him.

The incident convinced the sceptics that prompt and decisive action was vital. The cordon is to be set up right away and everyone will help to man it. No-one goes out and no-one comes in until we know what the hell's going on.

23rd March 1995

I spent the whole of last night sitting up with Jean. She was slipping in and out of consciousness the whole time. In her more wakeful moments, I tried to persuade her to go into hospital, but she was alert enough to refuse categorically.

There's something unbearably lonely about the wee small hours. I couldn't stop thinking about Audrey and my deplorable conduct in that department. And about the poor woman in hospital. Where will this all end?

About two o'clock in the morning, I decided I couldn't bear my thoughts spinning any longer. Activity was what was needed. Keep my mind off things. I found a large piece of paper and drafted a rota for manning the cordon. We need someone there twenty-fours hours a day to stop people getting out or in. I divided it into four shifts to spread the burden. This required military precision.

I knew who would be available – Mick Johnson, of course, Ron Dixon, Sinbad and one or two others. One name was missing – mine. I feel so torn. I ought to be with the troops. The chairman of the Brookside Residents' Association should be on the front line with his men, so to speak. But every time I tried to assign myself a shift, I thought of Jean lying there alone. Until she's on the mend, I cannot bear to leave her, even for four hours. I'm going to have to be a bit of a back-room boy on this one.

Mick Johnson popped round to see how Jean was doing this morning. I gave him the rota and explained the omission. He was a great comfort, telling me to leave everything to him and just worry about Jean and the rest of the family. A crisis really brings out the best in people.

If and when Barry Grant returns, he's going to get quite a surprise. Number 5 has become an unofficial refuge. Mick's moving in with his two youngsters. So is Jimmy Corkhill. It seems he got stuck behind the barrier. Serves him right for constantly trying to wheedle his way in where he's not wanted. His presence is not likely to make life any easier, however. Even if I'd known he was in residence, I wouldn't have included him on the cordon rota. The man would be accepting bribes for those wishing to leave before we could blink.

Mid-morning a large white vehicle, marked MOBILE MEDICAL UNIT, pulled up at the edge of the Close. The authorities have swung into action straight away. They've identified Mick Johnson as my deputy and given him details of what's required. Everyone is to provide urine and blood samples. Emma has kindly offered

Barry Grant's living room as a waiting area for the clinic. Ron and Beverley made a brief bid for freedom, as I rather feared they might, but Sinbad and Mick persuaded them to co-operate and they've returned home. The team spirit is back in the Close, thank God.

Harrowing conversation with Patricia this afternoon. She'd come back from the hospital briefly to change and, ostensibly, to rest, but she just stood at the window, staring at Thomas's slide, tears running down her face.

There's no disguising it – Thomas is deteriorating. His very life may be in danger. Max is still missing, travelling through America. We've left message after message, but there hasn't been a word. Patricia's going through hell. I hardly know what to say. She's consumed by fury at a world that can so decimate her family, after all they've been through with Alice. She's terrified her son will die and she's racked with guilt.

'I didn't mean it,' she said. 'It just came into my head, just for a moment. I thought that Thomas had more to live for than Alice. I wished it was Alice who was ill. I feel so guilty, because I wouldn't want anything to happen to her. I love her so much.'

As she sobbed in my arms, I realized that unconsciously I had thought exactly the same thing. May God forgive me and keep my precious granddaughter safe.

24th March 1995

When I went in to see Jean this morning, she seemed

much better, almost miraculously so. I can't persuade her to go into hospital, even though she's clearly still unwell. A small improvement convinces her she's over the worst. I'm not so sure.

I don't know how to put the latest tragic event on paper. I find myself desperately eager to record trivia. Such as Corkhill's attempt to escape and his recapture by our ex-soldier, Carl Banks, using SAS methods. Or how the milkman has to leave the milk fifty yards from the barrier. Or that the wallpaper is peeling by the dressing table and the weather stays calm.

Audrey is dead. Jean insisted I telephone the hospital for a progress check. They told me Audrey passed away yesterday evening. Simply stopped breathing. I considered keeping the news from Jean till she's better, but my face gave me away as soon as I went back to the bedroom. She took it very hard. I don't think she could quite believe it. Only minutes before, she'd been talking of Audrey as part of the family. I fear this is going to put her recovery back weeks.

I can't quite believe it myself. Audrey is dead. I put the words down again, but they still don't seem real. She'll never call me 'Major', will never smile at me in that special way, half-threat and half-enticement. For so many months, I've wished her out of my hair. Did I will her death? Did I really want it? I'd give anything to have her back. But now she's gone, along with our guilt-ridden liaison, which I so regret.

Who's it going to claim next? Where in God's name is it all going to end?

25th March 1995

I hardly slept last night. Only to be expected, of course. Spent the morning making a bonfire in the back garden. Burned Audrey's sheets from the spare room. Clutching at straws. Still, until we know what's causing this epidemic, anything's worth a go. It gave me something to do.

Emma arranged a small party at Barry's to rally the troops. It was a splendid idea. Just what we needed to pull everyone together. Jean almost had to throw me out to go there. I can hardly bear to leave her at the moment. She said I needed a change of scene.

I have to admit it was a relief to see the others. Unfortunately, I fear I made a bit of a fool of myself. With all that's been going on lately, I couldn't resist the temptation of a rather good drop of malt. I downed a couple and made my excuses. Everyone was so kind. One after another, they offered me words of comfort and support. I couldn't help it. Simply broke down and wept. In front of all my neighbours. I knew how damaging this must be to the troop's morale to see their leader in this state.

I got back to discover Jean had had a relapse. She'd collapsed on the sofa and was out for the count. I got her back to bed, then summoned an ambulance. When I returned from making the call, Jean had opened her eyes. I reassured her that help was on its way, but she said 'no', very quietly, but very firmly.

'I'm not going to hospital,' she said, still in that small, stubborn voice. 'I'm staying here with you.'

She made me go to the top drawer of her dressing table and fetch an envelope hidden inside. It was her living will – a piece of nonsense, I'd thought when she'd made it. I'd promised her then to abide by its conditions, because, frankly, I didn't take it seriously. It stated clearly that should Jean fall ill, she did not want to die in hospital, nor did she want to receive treatment.

'I want to die here,' she murmured. 'At home, with you.'

I'd given her my word. I had no choice but to send the ambulance away again.

26th March 1995

An uneasy night. I sat up with Jean, but kept dozing off. Everything seems unreal, except for the nightmares that come as soon as my eyelids close. Horrible dreams, full of guilt and despair. Muddled demons from hell.

Jean didn't sleep any more easily. She was burning up and coughing her heart out. The one thing that could be guaranteed to wake her up fully was any mention of the word 'hospital'. I managed to persuade her to see a doctor, but he just shook his head and said she should be where she can receive constant, professional medical attention. Unfortunately, there's no law in this country forcing people to do what's good for them. Even if there was, no doubt Jean would ignore it.

There is one glimmer of hope on the horizon. Max is back. He arrived late last night and went straight from the airport to his son's bedside. Our messages hadn't reached him for days. He'd been staying with some business associates and hadn't gone back to the hotel. So much for American efficiency. The hotel was supposed to pass on any messages immediately, but they didn't bother until the fourth one labelled URGENT was put through.

What really upset Max was seeing his son in an isolation ward. Patricia has had days to get used to the idea, but he couldn't bear it. In desperation, he pushed past the nurses and took Thomas in his arms. Of course, once he'd gone in, Patricia followed. The staff tried to stop them, but to no avail. They spent the next couple of hours in there, talking to him, letting him know he wasn't alone. They had put themselves at immense risk by potentially exposing themselves to the mystery virus. But Max didn't care. He just wanted to hold his son.

Then Thomas opened his eyes. Patsy said it was the most amazing sight. All of a sudden, his breathing seemed to become regular, his skin stopped feeling so clammy and his lips mouthed 'Daddy'. He's definitely on the mend. Patsy was calling from the ward's public telephone, so she couldn't fill me in on any more details. It was as if their heroic deed was being repaid.

I was so relieved, it brought the tears to my eyes. I can't believe how much a grown man has wept during these terrible times. The news brought comfort to Jean as well. She was so nearly unconscious, I wasn't sure if she heard, but she smiled and seemed to breathe more easily.

27th March 1995

I have to face it. Jean is near the end. She's slipped into a coma, from which I fear she will never wake. Max and Patricia are downstairs. Even though Thomas is still so ill, I felt I had to send for them. Patsy would never forgive herself if her mother slipped away before she had a chance to say goodbye.

I asked the children to let me have some time alone with my wife. I put the record player on. Her favourite tunes. The memories came flooding back. All those old fifties songs. Jean had a crush on Johnny Ray. Never could understand it – all that sobbing and crying. I remember the very first time I met her. It was at a New Year's Eve party in Bristol. She'd come with a chap in a Triumph sports car. I can still see her as she was then. Prettier than Deborah Kerr in a strapless dress with sequins on the bodice. All the men at the party wanted to be with her. They played Such A Night and I asked her to dance. I was so surprised when she said yes, I almost forgot to move my feet. We never looked back. Marrying Jean was the best thing I ever did. I thought I was the luckiest man in the world.

I rambled on to her, going over forty years of marriage. I told her how much I love her, how deeply I regret not being a model husband. Touch too much testosterone in the old tubes. That's all it was. It never meant anything. Never.

I found myself swearing that I'd been faithful for the last thirty years, ever since that fiasco with Patsy's maid.

Then, in the silence, I heard Jean take a laboured breath and I knew I couldn't lie. Not at the final hour.

I confessed everything. Poured out the whole sordid truth about me and Audrey. Told her over and over how sorry I am.

Jean didn't move. I don't know if she heard me or not. I had to leave the room - just for a few moments – to write this down. It's like a weight pressing down inside my chest. I'm going back to her now. I want to be with her at the end.

28th March 1995

I'm so exhausted I can hardly pick the pen up. My mind's in a whirl, my throat's parched and sore, my eyes itch. Yet, I'm – not happy, exactly – but perfectly calm. Serene, if you like.

I woke up early this morning with a jump. I hadn't meant to fall asleep beside Jean. When I touched her hand, it was cold and clammy. There was no sign of breathing. No movement at all. She'd drifted away without anyone to hold her hand. I couldn't even do that for her. I thought in the end, she'd been all on her own. I was completely devastated.

The world had never seemed as bleak as when I had to break the news to Max and Patricia. I found them curled up on the sofa in each other's arms. I felt such a pang of loneliness, I thought my heart would break.

Patricia went in to say goodbye to her mother. She

came back smiling. Smiling. She'd kissed Jean on the cheek and got the fright of her life when she opened her eyes.

It was a bloody miracle. How it happened I don't know. I swear one minute she was no longer with us and the next she was demanding tea and a wash. I was summoned to her bedside.

How can I describe my feelings at that moment? Amazed, delighted, confused, overjoyed. Then, horror and fear crept in. If someone's got a high temperature and is slipping in and out of a coma, could they hear everything you say? What if Jean had heard my ramblings and sordid confession.

Patsy told me not to worry. Whatever I'd confessed, the important thing is that Jean has survived and is going to get better. That's all that matters. It's over, she said.

Trouble is, I fear she may be only too right.

30th March 1995

The epidemic is officially over. The cloud, as far as the rest of the area is concerned, has passed. In my absence, Mick called a meeting of the B.R.A. to report on the medical team's latest dictum. He popped in to give me the glad tidings this afternoon.

The quarantine has been lifted. Adults can return to work and children to school on Monday. They're still analysing the samples taken from people's fridges and lavatories and the like, but they've found nothing suspicious so far, so it looks like the homes and drains are in the clear. The virus has gone, as quickly as it came.

Where the wretched thing came from in the first place remains a mystery. Another week's research may give us the answer, but, frankly, I doubt it. It's a fact that there are millions of unknown virus strains throughout the world. The medical profession cannot identify them all, nor be sure where, if and when another could strike. With modern-day travel, a mystery virus can travel from the depths of a rain forest to an unsuspecting community such as ours in twenty-four hours.

I am waiting for my personal death sentence to be passed. Jean left the bedroom to fetch herself a drink of water and found me snoozing in the armchair. She had this odd look on her face. I didn't know if it was amused or angry or simply not quite awake.

'Nice dream?' she asked. 'I had some fascinating dreams while I was ill. At least, I think they were dreams. Or were they. No, I don't think they can have been, because they were so extraordinarily vivid.' Then she smiled. A wry, bitter smile. 'There you were by the bed, telling me all about your sad little episode of adultery with Audrey. I heard every word, David. It wasn't a dream, was it?'

I couldn't think what to do. I just stared at her with my mouth wide open. Jean stood there staring back, obviously waiting for me to say something, but I was rendered totally powerless by the realization of what had happened. After a few moments, she sighed and went back to bed. I didn't dare go after her. I've ruined everything.

3rd April 1995

The whole weekend's come and gone and not a word from Jean. It's not that she's not talking to me. I'd find that easier to bear. At least I'd know where I stand. She's polite, friendly even, but it's as though I'm sharing the house with a distant acquaintance. Her health's improved tremendously. You'd hardly know she'd been ill – or that we'd ever been married.

What am I supposed to do? What am I supposed to say? What the hell does she want from me?

I feel like going down on my knees and begging her forgiveness. Telling her how sorry I am and how much I love her, but what's the use? I need some kind of lead from her. For once in my life, I simply don't know what to do.

The rest of the Close has got back to normal remarkably quickly after our recent emergency, although tempers remain uncertain. There was an article in the local rag quoting one of the medical team. Apparently, it's likely that the infection was brought in by George Manners following one of his jaunts abroad. Not that it proves anything. We're never likely to get a satisfactory answer. It'll be one theory after another.

The environmental health people were here again today to make a final check of the whole estate. They told me it was just an added precaution, nothing to be alarmed about. Ron and Eddie were not convinced, however. They approached me to insist on a B.R.A. meeting to get to the bottom of things. Everybody is in desperate need of reassurance. I was reluctant to take on the organization, given how awkward things are at home, but pressure was brought to bear.

I told Jean we're to host the masses tomorrow night. She said it was fine and gave me another of her brutal, bright, empty smiles.

4th April 1995

I couldn't bear it any longer. I had to get Jean to talk. She didn't make things easy for me, pretending she didn't know what topic I wanted to discuss.

I'd girded the old loins, ready for the fray, when the doorbell rang. It was Beth Jordache, delivering flowers from herself and her mother. I tried to prevent her from coming in, but Jean insisted. Frankly, I don't like that young lady in the house at the best of times, but at that moment, her presence was a disaster.

It's not just that she's a lesbian – although that makes me feel queasy enough – it's the fact that Jean had a similar experience. Even after all these years, I'm still jealous of a woman Jean had a close 'friendship' with before I'd even met her. I know it's ridiculous, but I simply can't help the way I feel. That sort of behaviour – well, it's just not natural, is it?

Jean was furious with me for being abrupt with Beth. Ironically, it could have been a good thing. At least, it got it off her chest. The words came pouring out.

'What's the matter with you? Don't you like the idea that there's a lesbian in the same room? Do you think I won't be able to contain myself? I know how your mind works. This may come as a surprise to you, but not everybody keeps their brains between their legs.'

I pointed out to Jean that I'd merely wanted Beth to leave so we could talk. She'd heard my confession about Audrey, but hadn't given me any kind of reaction. I needed to know if she'd ever be able to forgive me. In my heart, I'd realized the whole situation was hopeless. Her tirade was like a tidal wave.

'You only told me about Audrey because you thought I was going to die. You didn't do it for my benefit or for the sake of our relationship, but out of pure selfishness. You thought it would somehow make it easier for you to go on living if you had a clear conscience. If you were really so racked with guilt for all these months, why did you wait till I was on my deathbed before you made your sordid little confession? Over these past few days I've learned how precious life is. I am not going to let you or anyone else spoil what little time I might happen to have left, so if you have come here looking for forgiveness, you have come to the wrong person.'

With that, she put her hands on my shoulders, thrust me bodily out of the bedroom and slammed the door in my face.

5th April 1995

Have I made the right decision? Is there anything else I could have done?

After Jean's outburst, I spent the night on the spare bed. I would say slept there, only I couldn't even close my eyes. All I could do was lie there, facing the ruin of my marriage. Forty years down the drain because of one trivial, pathetic transgression.

I couldn't face Jean this morning. I kept well out of the way until the residents' meeting. Putting on a jolly face to the world must be one of the hardest tasks I've ever faced. It went well. I reported back on what the authorities had said, distributed one final set of sample bottles and arranged for flowers to be sent to the funerals for the deceased. There was a certain amount of anxiety, which was allayed. Sinbad ended the meeting on a cheerful note with an invitation to Rachel Jordache's sixteenth birthday party. At least, they can put their troubles to one side for a while.

When everyone had gone, Jean and I were left facing each other. Silence. Then Jean asked me if there was anything I wanted to get off my chest. What could I say? I asked her what she wanted to hear, but she said she wasn't going to write the script for me as well. I really don't understand women. It's like playing a guessing game, only no-one will tell me the rules.

In the end, I went off for a quick stroll to clear my head. Whilst I was out, I made a decision. There's only one thing for it. I'm going to do the decent thing. Leave.

As far as I can make out, that's what Jean's waiting for me to do. When I told her, she simply said 'oh'.

'Is that all you're going to say?' I asked.

'Why? Do you want me to persuade you to stay?' she replied.

OF COURSE, I DO. It must be perfectly obvious. But how can I have the temerity to demand such a thing? After all the pain I've caused her, she's better off without me. It's decided. I'll make a move first thing in the morning.

6th April 1995

Things didn't quite go to plan. I'm writing this in the spare room of Casa Bevron. Ron and Beverley are downstairs with the TV blaring out game show inanities at top volume. I can scarcely believe I've ended up here.

I got up before dawn to pack, then as soon as it was reasonable, made a call to Ted Bond. He said it was perfectly alright for me to stay with him and Marjory until I sort myself out.

Jean dismissed me with a wave of the hand. Hardly looked up from the *Times* crossword. She told me to drive carefully and that was that. As if I was off to the shops, not walking out of her life forever.

Before I departed from Liverpool, I had to say goodbye to Patsy. I found her at the flower shop – she's been taking over Jean's shifts while she's been ill. My heart nearly broke at the sight of her in the institutional green uniform.

Of course, she was horrified and distressed. How could it be otherwise? I desperately wanted to confide in her, but I knew if I did, I'd lose my daughter as well as my wife. Max hasn't always kept to the straight and narrow, so I'm well aware of Patricia's views on infidelity.

'You can't just walk in here out of the blue and tell me you're leaving,' she said. 'You've got to stay here and sort out whatever your problems are.'

If only it were that simple.

I had one final, miserable task. Under the circumstances, I cannot continue to be chairman of the Brookside Residents' Association. I must resign. I am no longer a resident. When I think of the amount of time and effort I've put into it. Starting it up, keeping it going through times of apathy and lack of interest. It proved its worth in this time of crisis and will go from strength to strength. It breaks my heart to think I have to abandon it at its height.

The only person I could think of to take over was Ron Dixon. He's a capable man and has always supported the B.R.A. He was noticeably touched when I asked him if he would shoulder the burden in my stead.

'It's a big honour,' he said. 'But no-one could run the B.R.A. the way you do.' I felt a lump emerge in my throat.

Before I left Liverpool behind me, I had to make a quick call to Ted to give him an E.T.A. Ron kindly allowed me to use his phone, as I felt awkward slinking back to the bungalow. Seemed there was a bit of a hitch. Marjory put her foot down. She didn't want to be seen to be taking sides between Jean and myself.

Which put me in a rather sticky situation. Turfed out of my own house and nowhere to go. I was about to go and find a hotel for the night, when Ron came up trumps. It's just for the night, however. Tomorrow I'll have to move on.

7th April 1995

I'm back at my old desk again. Thank God. Not that our troubles are over, but I think I can see light at the end of the tunnel.

First thing this morning, I contacted another old pal, Gilbert in Cambridge. He's single, so was perfectly prepared to put me up, no questions asked.

Unfortunately, I ran into Patricia as I was leaving Ron's. I told her firmly that 8am in the middle of the Close was neither the time nor the place for an in-depth discussion. The minx grabbed my car keys and refused to hand them over until I'd given her chapter and verse.

I had no choice. I had to make my confession about Audrey all over again. Patricia was furious. I can expect no sympathy from her. She tore me off several strips about my disgraceful behaviour. As if I wasn't fully aware of what I'd done. Not that I didn't deserve it. But my punishment was clear. Face life without Jean, if such an existence can be dignified by that term. I adore her. I always have. I'm nothing without her.

Patricia's view was that I should have been telling Jean all this, but I couldn't see the point. The damage had already been done. Nonetheless, Patsy refused to release my car keys until I'd made an effort to clear the air.

Effectively I was marooned. Ron reluctantly agreed to put me up for another night, but Bev was having none of it. I overheard them arguing in the kitchen. Bev said she was sick of having her house used as a hostel for the homeless. And I always thought she was such a nice girl.

I was still plucking up my courage either to face Jean or some grubby B&B when the doorbell rang. It was my wife, come to fetch me home. After all I'd done to her, the marvellous woman was still prepared to carry on.

The illness decided her. Flirting with death helped her put things into perspective, realize what's important and what isn't. What hurt her wasn't so much the thought of me with Audrey, but the deceit. That I'd thought I could get away with lying to her.

Worst of all, I'd run away. I see that now. I should have stayed and fought. We've been together for more than forty years and I'd been too weak even to discuss the matter with her.

I finally found out what she'd wanted from me. She'd wanted me to beg for forgiveness. She'd wanted me to tell her how much I love her. She'd wanted me to say I'd been a fool, that it was all a big mistake and that it would never happen again. Above all, she'd wanted me to say I was sorry. All the things I was dying to say, but couldn't.

So we carry on. I've promised to be absolutely honest with her and that I'll never run away from trouble again. I've learned my lesson. Next time, she won't come chasing after me.

8th April 1995

We have a guest – not an entirely welcome one from my point of view. Rachel Jordache. Whilst I was staying chez Casa Bevron, Jean went to Rachel's sixteenth birthday party. Apparently, all was going well until Mandy Jordache announced she's pregnant. Sinbad is the father, of course. It was quite a revelation. Rachel flew into the most terrible rage, shouting at her mother and even physically attacking her. Of course, one can understand it. The poor girl must have had a terrible shock.

The guests left hurriedly. Jean was the last to go. She was offering a few words of comfort to Mandy, when Rachel came banging down the stairs, suitcase in hand. She announced she was leaving home, never to return.

Jean stepped into the breach and offered her a bed for the night. What else could she do? Much as I resent having anyone else around at such a delicate time in our marriage, I do see she couldn't simply abandon the poor girl.

Unfortunately, it appears that her sojourn with us may be somewhat extended. I will say this for Ms Jordache, she is resourceful. Took herself off to the housing department and presented herself as homeless. Given her age, the powers that be have no choice but to find her accommodation. However, they consider their duties are fulfilled by bunging her in some kind of hostel. What sort of care is that for a vulnerable teenager, desperately traumatized by the tragic events in her family? Let's hope they can offer her something decent soon.

9th April 1995

Jean and I took Rachel to the Albert Dock this afternoon. It made a very pleasant outing. On the whole, our young guest was far better company than I had anticipated. Recent events have been so traumatic, it's hardly surprising she reacted with force. Now there's an oasis of calm, she's proving thoughtful and courteous, if somewhat quiet.

The poor old quayside has changed vastly since my young day. I suppose there's far more for modern youth. Rachel was very taken with the TV studio, then we took her to the shops. How women can spend an entire afternoon absorbed in bits of cloth, I will never be able to fathom. Then we stopped off in a cafe for a spot of well-earned tea, and Rachel cheered up immensely.

It seems a far cry from the days when I used to watch the great ocean liners. I miss them. There was something comforting about their sheer bulk. All that activity. Every time I quarrelled with Mother, I'd be down there, thinking things out. Rachel seemed fascinated by my stories of past times.

10th April 1995

Rachel's not a bad house guest. Polite, friendly, helps with the washing up and makes tea for everyone at the drop of a hat. However, having a young girl staying does bring its problems. It looks as though I'm just going to have to get used to it for the moment.

I was all set up for the weekly descent into the hell of the hypermarket with Jean, when she cried off. Thought she'd like to spend some time with our visitor. At the moment, I dare not disagree with any dictum from Jean. Her word is, literally, law around here. As well as our normal fare, she asked me to get a few things for Rachel. It's not that I object to that per se. The poor girl hasn't got a penny to her name and we are *in loco parentis*, so to speak. But she was in need of some items designed to aid a woman's travail each month. What on earth was Jean thinking of, expecting me, a mere man, to push a trolley round with those things on top of the cornflakes. I've never been so embarrassed in my life. The television's to blame. All those adverts showing articles with wings and cotton objects filled with blue ink has deprived the modern woman of any sense of decency.

Audrey's funeral, and young Gary's are being held tomorrow. The latter was a good friend of Rachel's – another tragedy for her to overcome. She really opened up to Jean this afternoon. The poor girl was in tears because she felt that without her father, she has little to live for. As she sees it, he was the only one who loved her. Beth and she do not get on and she cannot believe her mother loves her, with all her attention focused on Sinbad and the new baby.

Jean has told Rachel she can stay indefinitely. No discussion. I tried to protest, but under the circumstances I was on very shaky ground. We are currently abiding entirely by Jean's house rules. I have no say in anything.

11th April 1995

I have made a few tentative enquiries at the council concerning possible accommodation for a girl in Rachel's position. Given Jean's current state of mind, I had to do so with a certain amount of stealth. An extremely helpful chap gave me a list of bedsits and said they would help with the rent. The next stage is to persuade Jean to look at them with me.

We have to be practical. I fear Jean might be getting a little too involved. When all's said and done, Rachel is merely a neighbour. Besides, we need to make provision for the day when she tires of living with two old codgers. It looks like she may never want to go back to her mother. Someone has to think of the future.

Max and Patricia have a new project on. They've taken over the lease of the flower shop and are planning to turn it into something more upmarket. Precisely what they intend to stock is being kept a mystery, but it'll be some kind of gift shop. Patsy really is a chip off the old block. That girl's got enterprise.

12th April 1995

A traumatic day. I admitted to Jean what arrangements I'd made re Rachel and asked her to accompany me around the various council properties. At first, she was enraged, accusing me of wanting to offload a heart-broken young girl, who's put her total trust in us. She made me sound like a heartless monster, but I don't think it's a heinous crime to consider what the future might bring to said heartbroken young girl.

Strangely enough, it was Audrey's funeral that changed her mind. The service was well attended and all went smoothly, but such occasions invite one to reflect. Jean and I are entering that phase of our lives when death is a constant companion. Making contingency plans becomes a high priority.

After the funeral, we went to the first place on the council's list. Personally, I'd have given my eye teeth to be billeted in digs like that when I was sixteen. It contained a studio room, with separate kitchen and bathroom, not particularly clean and in need of some redecoration, but nothing that couldn't be fixed. Jean found it noisy, dark, depressing, cold and smelly.

In the end, our disagreements about the flat were pointless. We came home to find Rachel in tears. Gary's funeral had brought memories of her father flooding back. Worst of all, she blamed herself. What had she done wrong? Why was all this happening to her? All I could do was tell her over and over again that none of the dreadful events were even remotely her fault.

Seeing her sobbing in the kitchen made me realize Jean's right. Rachel's our responsibility now. As long as she's under our roof, however hard it is, we have to be as near as damn it mother and father to her. She needs us. It's as simple as that.

While Rachel was drying her eyes, I went exploring in the loft. I decided we'd had enough doom and gloom for one day. Patsy's old games and clothing were packed up there when we moved here. Scrabble was the order of the day. I've always relied on it to smooth over life's most difficult moments. I hate to admit it, but Rachel beat me into a cocked hat. Her triumph was the word 'zit' on a triple word score, clocking up a massive thirty-six points. Naturally, I challenged it on the grounds of colloquialism, but the *Concise Oxford English Dictionary*'s rarefied confines admitted the word.

Memories of Patsy roaring about the place came flooding back. As I recall, she used to hammer me at Scrabble as well.

14th April 1995

That loft is a veritable treasure trove. Rachel was highly amused by Patsy's old Bay City Rollers paraphernalia.

Goodness, that so-called song she played over and over and over again, until I thought my ears would literally burst. Something about 'Bang A Gang'.

Then there were the platform shoes. Jean and Patsy argued for a full week about them. Dangerous. Unfit for school wear. Not to mention unutterably hideous. Curiously enough, Rachel liked them. Apparently, they're now considered trendy. Some things never change.

There's a hell of a lot of stuff up there. At some point, I really must continue my expedition to see what other treasures can be discovered.

It was the grand opening of the Gift Box this afternoon. Patricia and Max did a terrific job. Put their hearts and souls into it. They'd got a fire eater, a juggler, a bouncy castle for the children and wine for the adults. The shop itself looked marvellous. All sorts of unusual knick knacks and gewgaws. Patricia has a real eye for design. Her displays were sumptuous. Of course, on the first day, people weren't buying a great deal. They'd merely come to investigate. No doubt they'll be back. Good taste is a requirement for all.

I excused myself early on the grounds that I had a mission to accomplish. I went in search of posters of the latest hip cats on the hit parade to brighten our new lodger's room up a bit. The trip was quite an ordeal. I had to interrogate a somewhat taciturn youth with frightening orange hair for the best part of half an hour. Once I'd worked out how to decipher his primeval grunts, he was quite helpful. He recommended

America's leading exponents of grunge music.

I found Rachel in her room going through more of Patricia's old things with Lee Banks. She received the poster with good grace, but little enthusiasm. I couldn't help hanging around outside the door to suss out what she really thought. Apparently, my tangerine-haired anarchist gave me a bum steer. Rachel described the persons depicted on the poster as 'sad smellies'. Frankly, I was rather relieved she didn't identify with them.

When Rachel came out of her bedroom, I told her she need not put the posters up. She was utterly charming about the whole thing. Said there was nothing wrong with them, but that she herself wasn't into that sort of stuff. She then made a little speech saying how kind we'd been and how grateful she is for being treated as part of the family. Who says that modern youth has no manners?

15th April 1995

Rachel slipped back to her mother's to collect the rest of her belongings today. Unfortunately, she got the shock of her life. Her bedroom had been turned into a nursery for the new baby and her stuff was in the extension room downstairs. She was devastated. Sinbad and Mandy arrived back moments later, to find her storming out in tears.

They tried to explain, but Rachel was much too upset to listen. Sinbad had turned the extension into a bedsit, fit for the most independent teenager. The nursery was an afterthought, only Rachel couldn't see it that way. She screamed that she'd rather live with the Yorkshire Ripper than stay at number 10. She's back at the bungalow now, locked into the spare bedroom. I put my ear to the door earlier and heard her sobbing.

Mandy and Sinbad had some more news to tell. The trial date has been set. On Monday, 8th May 1995, Amanda and Elizabeth Jordache will be answering the charge of murder.

16th April 1995

A day of turmoil. Rachel announced that she does not intend to go back to school. No amount of argument will change her mind. I can't bear to see her give it up like this. She's due to take her GCSEs at the end of July. The last five years at school have been leading up to them. Her teachers will make allowances for what's happened and the considerable amount she's missed. She's a bright girl. I'm sure she could pass.

Unfortunately, Rachel is convinced to the contrary. As far as she's concerned, she's bound to fail. She's also certain that her mother and sister are going to prison. In that event, she'll need money and accommodation, so her only hope is to get a job as soon as possible. It's a tragedy that she should be forced to be so cynical at her age.

Mandy called round with a letter that had come for

Rachel. I think it was partly an excuse. Rachel has refused all contact with her family and wouldn't come out of her bedroom. I pleaded with her to change her mind, but she was determined to avoid her mother at all costs. The poor girl must have been desperate. Whilst I knocked at her door, she was making her escape through the window.

She raced across the Close just as Eddie Banks came roaring round the corner on his Hog – or Harley Davidson to the uninitiated. He swerved to avoid her and was thrown into the bushes. Luckily, he was unhurt, apart from the shock and a cut on the leg. By the time we'd dusted him down and checked his beloved machine, Rachel was nowhere to be seen.

I had an idea where she might have gone. The Albert Dock. I persuaded Mandy to remain where she was and set off in hot pursuit. My guess was right. I caught up with Rachel gazing across the water, the picture of misery. It's a wonderful place to sort things out. Rachel and I talked for hours, mostly about my past and the difficulties I faced with a father dead in the war and a mother with whom I did not always see eye to eye.

Finally, Rachel agreed to return to the bungalow. However, she made one condition. I had to promise she wouldn't have to speak to her mother if she didn't want to. Under the circumstances, I agreed. I felt terribly guilty having to tell Mandy she couldn't speak to her own flesh and blood, but I had no option. All I could do was ask her to bear with me whilst I try and talk Rachel round.

17th April 1995

In all the furore of yesterday, we totally forgot the letter Mandy delivered. It was from the Crown Court. Rachel had been summonsed to appear as a witness – for the prosecution. They want her to give evidence against her mother and sister.

You could have knocked me over with a feather. I insisted Rachel tell us what's going on. I rather wish I hadn't asked. Apparently, Mandy and Beth told the police that Trevor Jordache molested his daughters. First Beth and then Rachel. It was the latter that proved the final straw for Mandy, leading to the plot on his life.

Rachel denies it categorically. Why should she lie? Mandy and Beth could have cooked the whole story up to gain the sympathy of the jury. I certainly wouldn't put it past Madam Beth, although it's only fair to record that Jean considers this mere prejudice on my part. Neither of us can see Mandy making up something like that.

Yet the man was a monster. A violent brute. I find it far easier to believe he was a molester than that Mandy Jordache is a cold-hearted killer. If what she and Beth say is true, then that loathsome individual deserved all he got. The idea of him laying his filthy hands on Rachel is almost too much to bear.

19th April 1995

I'm worried about the Gift Box. I was helping out

today and couldn't help noticing there were a lot more boxes of stock coming through the door than customers. Surely they should have a few more customers, even in these early days. Not that it's any of my business.

I have made a large impulse purchase. Eddie Banks was more shaken up by the accident than I thought. The net result is that he's decided to sell his Harley Davidson. I'm astonished he can part with it. He's out there every weekend, polishing and tinkering with the insides, lavishing love and affection on it.

I must say it's a superb piece of mechanical engineering. When I heard it was up for grabs, I had a vision of the wind in my hair, roaring out on to the open road. But I knew it was just a pipedream as Jean would have put her foot down. Rachel was much more behind me. I only went for a little peek, but her young, infectious enthusiasm soon had me sold on the idea, putting all thoughts of Jean's disapproval out of my mind. It was a bargain at £3,500. I could sell it tomorrow for a fat profit. Eddie and I shook hands on the deal straightaway. Jean is not best pleased.

20th April 1995

A most enjoyable morning spent with my new bike. Rachel is anxious to go for a ride, but I feel it will take a couple of days yet before we're ready. I've arranged for the insurance. Strictly speaking, I'm covered from the moment I made the call, but I do like anything legal to be absolutely tickety boo.

I sat on the saddle and revved her up. The power of the machine is quite incredible. A veritable bucking bronco. I was about to set off, when I noticed one or two tiny details that really need fixing before I actually get on the open road. After what happened to Eddie, a very experienced rider, I can't be too careful. Safety first has always been my motto. Of course, I'm sorry to disappoint Rachel and sorry myself that I can't get this monster out on the open road.

We went to see the Crown Prosecution Service's solicitor this afternoon. Jean and I were allowed to accompany Rachel as temporary guardians. It was a terrible ordeal for her, having to go over and over what happened. All those sordid details. She stuck to her story – insisting her father never touched her. I hate to think what's going to happen in the witness box when she comes up against a smart aleck barrister. There's nothing we can do, except give her as much support as we can.

When we came home, Rachel asked again to go out on the bike. I must admit (and only within the confines of these pages) that I may have been a little rash with this purchase. It's not that I don't like the thing, it's just that it's more powerful and, well, bigger than I'd imagined. I made excuses to Rachel once again, avoiding Jean's look.

21st April 1995

I've had to say farewell to the old Harley. Rosie came round to see Jean and confided that Eddie had made a dreadful mistake. It was simply slaughtering him to see his beloved bike in another's hands. I know how much he dotes on it. He's nearly as fond of it as I am of my Cortina. I'd be heartbroken if I had recklessly sold it and had to watch a neighbour driving off in it every day. I cannot do it to a friend. I swear Eddie had tears in his eyes when I returned it.

I do still quite fancy a Harley Davidson, but perhaps not just at the moment. Rachel is extremely keen. She bought a motorbike magazine and spent the afternoon scouring the small ads. However, the project is shelved for the moment. Jean would never agree and she is, after all, the boss.

There was one good side effect, however. Rachel has discovered an ambition. The magazine she was reading contained an article about a girl mechanic and the job appealed to her straight away. Immediately, Jean and I pointed out that she'd need her GCSEs to do something like that. Vehicles are much more complicated these days. Rachel readily agreed to go back to school next term and get a few qualifications. She mentioned something like, 'Just like Kylie off *Neighbours*.' I sometimes think today's youth talk in some form of code.

I've finally got around to clearing out all the junk from the garage and loft. Jean, as usual, wanted the lot dumped, but there were some items in extremely good condition. Just as I was trying to make up my mind what to do, Jacqui Dixon, Ron's daughter, came up. It seems she's trying to make a few extra coppers by going to car boot sales. Only snag is that she hasn't got a car. We've agreed to make a jaunt to Preston next week, using my Cortina and her sales technique. She'll sell our jumble for a share of the profits. A most satisfactory solution.

24th April 1995

Rachel went off to her new school this morning. I must say she looked just the ticket in a dark blazer and smart skirt. Even though she's sixteen, there's something terribly young and vulnerable about her. It actually gave me a bit of a pang to see her go. First day and all that.

Jean and I had a quiet word with her form and head teachers. They'd heard about the trial, like everyone else in Liverpool, and were extremely understanding. Rachel will be given as much time and extra attention as possible. Of course, with the degeneration of our entire education system, I fear that intentions will far outstrip what's possible in practice.

I spent the day packing stuff up, ready for the boot sale tomorrow. Jean was at the Gift Box most of the afternoon, but managed to get back just before Rachel. It was all too easy for her to get away. There simply aren't the customers coming through the door.

Rachel was tired, but reported that school went well.

The other students were naturally curious about her mother and sister. Ironically, the affair gave her a certain cachet amongst her new chums. She was quite taken with her teachers too, especially the apparently handsome young history master.

I felt positively ancient when Rachel told me the period she'd be studying is the Second World War. I do have a lot of memories of the time, albeit as a child. Her text book had a section in it about the celebrations at the end of the war. Pictures of parades and street parties and that sort of thing. I remember them well.

Then Rachel had an excellent idea. VE Day is a mere fortnight away. The nation is planning to celebrate. She suggested that we hold a street party in the Close. It's the very place, simple to close off, a tight-knit community. As chairman of the B.R.A., I'll be only too happy to organize it. I don't think I'll bother with a meeting, however. Every time I try to call one nowadays, people always seem to have prior engagements.

The only snag is my own personal history. Patricia has spilled the beans about my father being a major in the war. Of course she's proud of her grandfather. So proud, I've never been able to face telling her the truth.

25th April 1995

Never again. Ron Dixon wants to keep his daughter in order. Jacqui and her friend, Katie, were round at the crack of dawn, ostensibly to help me load up the car. In reality, they examined the goods, giggling at my possessions, while I did the hard work.

We arrived in Preston and found a spot. Before I had time to blink, the two girls had swanned off, leaving me to set up and staff our outlet alone. Despite promising to be no more than five minutes, they turned up two and a half hours later. By that time, my throat was parched from lack of refreshment, my feet were exhausted from having to remain standing up and my bladder was, not to put too fine a word to it, bursting.

After all that effort, we had to take a good half of the stuff back with us. Jacqui Dixon spent the entire journey back trying to persuade me to give her driving lessons. The little madam had the cheek to suggest it would mean she could borrow my car. As if I'd let that manipulative chit come within six feet of the steering wheel! That's the last time I allow myself to be pressganged.

Sinbad called round, ostensibly to thank Jean and myself for persuading Rachel to go back to school. The hidden item on his agenda was to try to have a word with her. Apparently, things are looking grim for Mandy and Beth. Rachel's testimony will be vital to the trial. Sinbad's worried that, being so young, she hasn't thought through the implications of what she's saying about her father.

I was absolutely on the horns of a dilemma. I've a lot of time for Sinbad and I know he means well, but if it got back to the powers that be, it could backfire hideously on those wretched women.

At the end of the day, Rachel is a child who need protection. Jean and myself have been entrusted with her well being. We're her guardians. This pressure could tear her apart and I cannot allow that to happen.

26th April 1995

I donned my smartest suit and treated myself to a Union Jack and a jaunty plastic bowler, decked in the old red, white and blue in order to rally the troops to the street party. Everyone has been gratifyingly enthusiastic. I started off chez Banks. With young Carl having been in the army, I knew they'd be keen. Carl even promised to provide a substantial amount of beer at virtually pre-war prices for the refreshments section. I knew I could rely on an ex-military man.

Ron and Mick have promised to be there, as has Jackie Corkhill, Ron's trusty assistant. Her husband may be one of the biggest miscreants it has ever been my misfortune to meet, but her only fault is her taste in men. She is a most agreeable and attractive woman. We were discussing the event in the Trading Post, when someone had the bright idea of dressing up. Jackie and Rosie Banks are all set to appear as the Andrews Sisters – as long as nobody expects them to sing. Patricia said she'd be the third. So, unfortunately, did Beverley. I don't suppose it'll matter if we have four Andrews Sisters. The more the merrier.

Ron was banging on about his father. Seems he was some kind of a hero, with a chest full of gongs. Killed fifteen men single-handed. According to him, they practically had to open a medal factory, just to keep up with Dixon Senior. I found myself perpetuating the dreadful lie I've told all these years. How can I let the truth out at a time like this?

There is the anti brigade, of course. Max refused to have anything to do with it, to my surprise. Jacqui Dixon was completely uninterested and her brother, Michael, was positively vituperative. Claimed that celebrating the war was sick. He simply doesn't understand. A lot of men and women who fought in the war would be delighted if they knew we were drinking their health. They died to prevent this country being overrun by hoards of murdering Nazi thugs.

26th April 1995

How can I look my fellow citizens in the face? What would Ron Dixon say if I told him the truth? That my father was a coward. A whey-faced lily-liver. A pacifist. How could I ever look Patricia in the face again? How can I tell her that the grandfather she's so proud of was nothing more than a conscientious objector, sent down a pit because he refused to fight for his country.

I won't blight her life as mine has been. Why should she have to suffer the stigma? Other children had fathers who were killed in the war. At least they had a hero to remember. Or the fathers came back to pick up where they left off. What was I left with? A father buried in

Cornish coal and a pillowcase full of white feathers. Thanks to him I spent my school days bullied and beaten and ignored. He put his principles before his family and I can never forgive him for that.

27th April 1995

That wretch, Corkhill, has wormed himself an invitation to our celebrations on the extremely flimsy pretext that he is caretaking Barry Grant's place. God knows what he'll turn up in. More welcome guests will be Sinbad and Mandy Jordache. Probably need cheering up with the trial so imminent. I just hope we don't end up with tabloid photographers crawling all over the place again.

I had a bright idea for our centrepiece. Carl Banks is going to try to arrange for a tank to be delivered to the Close. Having such good connections with the military, I'm sure he'll be able to come up with the goods, even if it's one of those inflatable jobs they use on exercises.

Ron Dixon's display of his father's regalia is really quite impressive. I was forced to elaborate my nefarious piece of fiction regarding my own parent. It's all getting so concrete. To stop the questions about why there are no photos or medals, I implied that his work was a bit hush hush. Major Crosbie, head of special operations. How on earth am I going to get out of this one?

Lying to Patricia is the worst thing. Jean urged me to come clean, but I can't let Patricia down like that. How can I tell her that her grandfather was a coward and her father's a liar?

29th April 1995

A most extraordinary encounter today. I was putting an invitation to the street party through the Jordaches' letter box, when Beth flung the door open. She waved a letter under my nose, postmarked Preston, then proceeded to interrogate me as to my exact actions whilst in that god-forsaken hell hole.

I assured her I sent no letters from there. I didn't even go near a post box. She actually wanted me to prove it! My word wasn't good enough. Sinbad came out and explained that for several weeks, Mandy and Beth have been receiving hate mail on a regular basis. It seems some anonymous psychopath has been sending death threats. On one occasion, there was even a lethal dose of sleeping pills taped to the envelope. What has become of society?

It was unbelievable. I was astonished and appalled that Beth could think I was capable of such vicious, sick acts. I may not approve of her lifestyle, but I have told her so openly. For God's sake, Jean and I are on her and her mother's side, whatever Beth's sexual inclinations.

In the end she believed me, but the whole incident has shaken me severely. As I walked back to the bungalow, she was yelling her innocence to the world. Let's hope it convinces a jury. Although, I fear with such a temper, Beth may only make things worse.

2nd May 1995

Preparations for the party well underway. One slight hitch. The beer promised by Carl Banks was delivered by a large lorry. I was most impressed by the sheer quantity, until I read the labels. No wonder it was so cheap. Brewed in Germany! I couldn't believe it! An insult to every British soldier that died in the war. We can't celebrate VE Day with German beer. I ordered Carl dispose of the lot and spent a good deal of the afternoon arranging for an alternative supply. The inflatable tank, however, looks splendid. An ideal centrepiece. Completely makes up for the hiccup over the alcohol.

The troops have turned out in droves. Just about everyone on the Close has spent an hour or two on bunting patrol. The Close is really starting to take on a festive air. We're well on schedule to have everything prepared for the big day.

Seeing the Close so gay brought the old memories flooding back. I found myself getting positively maudlin thinking of all the young men who didn't come home. The devastated families. Thousands of people killed in the blitz. What a waste of humanity. Never again, we said at the time, but there are still wars the whole world over. Humanity wastes itself over and over again. Will we ever learn?

Ron is really getting into the spirit of the thing. You can hardly see the merchandise in the Trading Post for Union Jacks and patriotically coloured balloons. He's got a very special offer on for the big day. Any of his older customers that can produce their original ration books will be able to purchase goods for 1945 prices. I thought this remarkably generous, until Jackie Corkhill pointed out that the likelihood of anyone having kept their ration books is extremely small. Her guess is that Ron won't even get one brought in.

Patsy and Ron are still trying to persuade me to drag my father into the limelight. I find myself making the most ridiculous pronouncements. I actually told Ron that I couldn't put photographs of my father alongside his because Dad was an officer and it wouldn't do to have him on parade with the ranks. The conscientious objector has now become a stickler for military protocol and standards.

I was most impressed with Carl's efforts in replacing the offending German lager, until I found it was merely the same stuff with the labels removed. However, at this late hour, I fear I must be forced into accepting this compromise. I just hope the residents can swallow it.

4th May 1995

Trust Jimmy Corkhill to put a fly in the ointment. The wretched philistine completely ruined my day. I merely asked him if he'd mind helping to set out the bar, pointing out that everyone else is doing their bit, when he turned on me. He actually accused me of not pulling my weight. 'Dishing out the orders like some flaming what-sit' were his exact words. The nerve of the man! Especially after he insisted on an invitation much against my better judgement.

Everything's ready for tomorrow's big day. The cars normally parked on the road have been removed. We've set up one long table right across the middle of the Close. The bar is opposite the bungalow in the shade of the tank.

Ron gave me a bit of a nasty turn, quite inadvertently. He's invited a couple of extra guests. Ex-army personnel from the Legion. Real old troopers who actually fought in the war. Of course, he was absolutely right to invite them, but I can foresee trouble. If only I hadn't pretended my father was a member of a local regiment. Someone's bound to blow the gaffe.

Poor old Ron has had his comeuppance over his special offer. The word's spread throughout the pension clubs of Liverpool, courtesy of Julia Brogan. Hoards of over-sixties descended on the Trading Post, waving ration books and demanding cut-price baked beans and chocolate bars. He was cleaned out in half an hour.

5th May 1995

Extraordinary the way things turn out. The party started off with a bang. Everyone really got into the spirit of the thing. I must say the costumes were marvellous. Jean wanted me to go as Churchill, but I didn't want anyone to think I was mocking the great man. My officer's uniform was far more appropriate. Sinbad, however, did come as our noble leader. I must say he looked the part. He certainly has the figure for it. Rachel made a convincing evacuee with her hair in bunches and a forlorn luggage label round her neck. Jean hunted out a pair of dungarees and a check scarf to dress up as a land girl. Very fetching. The Andrews Sisters – all four of them – were delightful. Then there was Mick as a rather dashing American GI, Eddie the ARP warden and, finally, Ron the spiv. Given the fiasco of yesterday, the latter seemed highly appropriate.

The trouble came when Alfie Doyle from the local branch of the Legion arrived. Of course it immediately came to light that there was no Major Crosbie in any local regiment. Patricia refused to believe the poor old man, until I broke down and confessed to everyone exactly what my father had been. I told how he served his country, not as some hero of a commanding officer but at the coal-face. Ron summed it up rather well, 'You mean he was a miner, not a Major?'

I couldn't face the looks of disgust and horror. I slipped back to the bungalow, ready to resign as chairman of the B.R.A. Patricia followed me. I expected remonstrances, anger, disgust even, but I have a far more understanding and tolerant daughter than I deserve.

She saw her grandfather's actions in a totally new light.

'He wasn't a coward,' she said. 'He was prepared to stand up for whatever he believed in. Whatever the cost. He was a man of principle. I'm proud of him.'

Patricia went on to liken his actions to those of the brave students who stood up to the tanks in Tiananmen Square. As she was well aware, I have nothing but admiration for those people. I'd never thought of it like that before. It must have taken a hell of a lot of guts for my father to stick to his beliefs. We were fighting fascism, but he was fighting his own war.

For the first time in my life, I actually started to admire him. He was only an ordinary office worker. I wonder how he coped with being sent down a coal mine in the middle of nowhere. It must have been a nightmare for him. In his own way, he genuinely was a hero.

We went back to the party to find Ron completely dismayed. Alfie Doyle had more than one revelation to make. He may not have known Major Crosbie, but he remembered the brave Cyril Dixon. He was in the catering corps. As for the fifteen people he was supposed to have slaughtered with his bare hands, he did that alright – poisoned them with his beef stew.

6th May 1995

Rachel had a visitor this afternoon. Her Auntie Brenna. Apparently, Rachel had written to her in Ireland, but had forgotten to tell us. She seemed a pleasant enough woman and her niece was overjoyed to see her. Jean and

I were pleased, too. With the trial starting on Monday, Rachel could do with some family support.

I made rather a gaff. Thinking Brenna must be Mandy's sister, I told her how glad she'd be to see her, after what that brute of a husband had done. There was a long and ominous silence.

'That brute of a husband is my brother,' Brenna said finally.

I've never been so embarrassed in my life. Under the circumstances, I naturally assumed Brenna belonged to Mandy's side. I can't help wondering why she's here. I hope it's simply for Rachel's sake.

I left the two of them to have a chat, but couldn't help overhearing a word or two of their conversation. Brenna was exhorting Rachel to stand up for her father, as he's not here to defend himself. I'm not sure she should be putting that kind of pressure on. Poor Rachel was in tears. Yet, she insists over and over again that Trevor never laid a finger on her and that he loved her.

7th May 1995

The Jordache trial is scheduled to begin tomorrow. Jean bought a large bunch of flowers for Mandy and Beth to wish them luck. I raised the objection that it could be seen as us taking sides. We really ought to be nailing our colours to Rachel's mast.

There was an awkward moment when Rachel wanted to know who the flowers were for. Jean covered up by saying they were for a friend in need of cheering up. Which was hardly a lie. I'm pleased to report she had the grace to look somewhat shame-faced when Rachel praised her as 'dead nice' and 'brill'.

Brenna visited again this evening. Frankly, I don't trust her. The woman is distinctly insinuating. She said she'd been getting lonely, sitting in a hotel room by herself. Memories of her brother came flooding back. Still, Rachel needs all the comfort she can get, especially from her family. What she doesn't need is Brenna Jordache's pep talk about not letting her father down. Can she really not have known what he was like?

I dread to think what tomorrow's going to bring.

8th May 1995

The trial has opened. I'm utterly exhausted – and this was only the first day. It's the start of what I'm sure will be a harrowing few days – weeks even. Rachel was notified that she won't be required to give evidence until tomorrow. After a lot of soul-searching, she decided not to go today. Jean stayed with her. I decided it was vital that one of us should be in attendance, so I went along with Mick Johnson and sat in the public gallery.

We had to dodge TV cameras and photographers outside the crown court. When we got inside, all was chaos. Not a soul had a clue what was going on. For an important case like this, surely they should have laid on more than one usher? He was an offhand, rather sarcastic individual, whose only word of advice was to stick to the coffee in the cafeteria. (Although it has to be admitted, he was right. Whoever was responsible for the tea should be locked up for life.)

The trial was due to start at 10am sharp. We didn't even get into the courtroom until gone noon. The judge, apparently, was tied up on another case. It was outrageous. Everyone concerned with the case – defendants, witnesses and onlookers – was stuck in the wretched little buffet, fighting for chairs. Our whole legal system seems to be creaking under the strain.

Sinbad, Mandy and Beth were sitting with their solicitor, a rather attractive young lady. Their barrister looks like a solid, intelligent sort of bloke. The defendants were obviously suffering from pre-trial nerves. Beth, unfortunately, reacted with sulks and temper. She actually had the nerve to accuse me loudly and abusively of sightseeing! As if it wasn't vital that I know what was going on in order to be able to support Rachel and report back to the other concerned residents. (Although I do think Beverley turning up with her camera was taking things too far.)

Brenna Jordache put in an appearance. There was some sort of brouhaha between her and Mandy in the ladies'. I'm not sure what was going on, but the result was that Beth actually attacked her aunt, knocking her to the floor. She landed on a trolley full of dirty crockery, sending plates, cups and cutlery all over the room. I hope Beth will control herself better on the stand. No judge worth his salt is going to tolerate that sort of outburst. She'll be considered in contempt.

Eventually, proceedings got underway. The atmosphere was incredible, like sitting in a pressure cooker. Ostensibly, the mood was calm. The dramatic speeches with lawyers stalking round the court, shouting 'OBJECTION' and 'OVERRULED' belong strictly to the television. This was the real thing. No sight of Cavanagh Q.C. or Columbo here. I was surprised at the long pauses, whilst the usher muttered to the judge or various bits of paperwork were sorted out. It was boredom of the most excruciating kind. Every minute's delay seemed to bode ill for Mandy and Beth, even though it meant nothing of the sort.

First of all, the jury was sworn in, then the charges were read. My heart went out to those two poor women in the dock. They were so mercilessly alone, separated by glass and a heavy wooden rail from their solicitor and all their supporters. Sinbad, being a witness, was not allowed in court. Beth had gone from defiant lesbian to vulnerable girl. She could scarcely see over the bar. Mandy sat absolutely rigid. I barely saw her move the entire day.

On the front bench, as it were, were the defence and prosecution counsels. Our chap is a Mr Anderson QC and the enemy is Mr Tate. Behind them sat Alison Dicks, Mandy and Beth's solicitor.

The charges were read and the defendants pleaded not guilty. Then Mr Tate made his opening speech. It's amazing how a single set of facts can be seen in totally opposing ways. The case he is to present concentrates on intent. Mandy and Beth meant to kill Trevor in cold blood.

It is surely going to be hard to prove otherwise. Trevor Jordache died of a single stab wound in the back. According to the prosecution, this was 'hardly the handiwork of a distraught mother trying to protect her daughter. It was the blow of the clinical assassin'. He was attempting to drag Mandy's character through the mire, prejudice the jury against her before a single witness has been heard. The portrait he painted was of a calculating, scheming Jezebel. Anyone who's ever spoken to Mandy would realize how ridiculous such a picture is. But the jury haven't had that opportunity and I'm not sure they'll get a chance in that place.

The real shock was that before stabbing the wretch, Beth and Mandy tried to poison him. Traces of weed-killer – dinitrophenol – were found in his liver. The stuff's been withdrawn from sale precisely because it is so dangerous, although plenty of people have old stock lying around their garden sheds. The women admit to mixing it with Trevor's whisky. Unfortunately, the stuff is tasteless in alcohol and Beth, as a medical student, might have known that.

So much for the murder. Tate then went on to the conspiracy charge: an agreement between parties to commit murder, where the parties concerned intend to carry out that murder. I fear it will be all too easy, under the circumstances, to make that one stick.

The rest of the day was taken up by expert witnesses. When I heard Mr Anderson cross-examine, I started up a touch from the depths of despair. The toxicologist described the poisoning as 'incompetent'. Only a teaspoonful was needed for a fatal dose, an amount that could have proved undetectable. In fact, almost five times that amount was administered – an overdose that points to an act of desperation.

The forensic expert was fascinating. He put together the events of that fateful night second by second, using the evidence of single hairs, traces of plastic bin-bag and pinpricks of blood still in the house after all these months. Trevor was stabbed in the kitchen with a large domestic knife taken from the cutlery drawer. He was then dragged into the extension, where he was wrapped in the infamous black bin-bags. From there, probably some days later, he was buried under the patio.

The plethora of clues were pounced on by the defence. Surely these cold-blooded assassins, who were by no means unintelligent, would have made some attempt to clear up after themselves. The forensics bod was positively gleeful – it was evident whose side he was on.

'If you want to get rid of someone properly, then there are a few rules worth following,' he told the court. 'A, Don't stab the victim in your own kitchen. B, Don't have them lodging in your extension while you're deciding what to do with them. It was hardly the crime of the century.' Well put, Sir!

Our sibling police officers took the stand next. DI Coburn described a hellish three days of interrogation after a terrifying week on the run in Ireland. How could he expect to get straight answers after all they'd been through? It seems that they confessed to everything. Surely such an admission must stand them in good stead.

PC Coburn, our community bobby on the beat, although intending to be on our side, unfortunately gave the most damning evidence heard today. He had visited the Jordaches when Trevor went missing. Unfortunately, he couldn't remember anything being out of the ordinary, apart from an overpowering stench. This was due to the body decomposing, but he was told it was the drains. Mrs Jordache, he said, didn't seem any more anxious than usual. What he failed to point out was that the woman was continually on edge. Having lived for twenty years with that monster, her nerves were permanently destroyed. How could he not have seen that?

The final prosecution witness was Brenna Jordache. A character witness for the deceased. I don't trust that woman further than I could throw her. She described him as 'a loving father, husband and brother'. As I might describe myself as the Queen of Sheba. She then went on to tell the most extraordinary pack of lies – how Trevor had changed in prison, how he'd rediscovered his religion, how he'd come to understand what made him so angry. As if it was Mandy's fault that he'd beaten her, but now he was full of Christian forgiveness. It was all I could do to keep my seat. I met the man. I saw the vicious, cruel look in his eyes and the terror in Mandy's. He hadn't changed. He'd come back deliberately to continue bullying, beating and abusing his family.

9th May 1995

Rachel had to take the stand today. Jean was up all night with her, trying to calm her down. The poor girl is so obviously torn. She continues to deny that her father did anything wrong, at least by her, yet she knows that denial could send her mother and sister to prison for a very long time.

Seeing her up there, alone in the witness box, brought the tears to my eyes. It was as if she shrank in age from a personable, mature sixteen-year-old to a shy child of six. Her voice got higher, quieter, more breathy. The picture of vulnerability. No-one could doubt for a minute that she was telling the truth.

Prosecution, defence and judge were as gentle with her as possible. Mr Tate went first. He took her carefully through those last tragic weeks. Whatever the rights and wrongs of the case – one thing's for sure, Rachel has been a victim all the way along the line. To cover up Trevor's death, Mandy told Rachel that he didn't want to live with the family any more and that he'd gone for good. Then by an amazing coincidence, the police found the decomposing corpse of some forlorn John Doe. Mandy took her chance and identified it as that of her supposedly missing husband. I remember the funeral. Rachel in tears throughout, Beth breaking down in the pulpit and unable to finish the lesson. I thought at the time how grief-stricken she seemed. God knows what was really going through her mind.

Rachel sounded so bitter when she spoke of how she

found out the truth about that ceremony.

'I couldn't believe it. My Mum had made me go to some tramp's funeral and sat there watching me cry my eyes out for my Dad.'

Mr Anderson proved his worth with the way he handled the questioning. He asked her if she thought it was up to her to protect her father's memory.

'Someone's got to stick up for him,' she replied.

The response to this was very clever. 'I'm sure any loving daughter would feel the same,' he said. 'But you have to remember that this is a court-room and you're under oath to tell the truth. You have to watch out for the point at which protecting someone means lying on their behalf.'

Is Rachel protecting her father? She told the court how Trevor would sneak up to her room, put his arm round her and tell her all his troubles. They cuddled, but she said over and over again that nothing whatever happened apart from that. Counsel for the defence went over what incest is and what statutory rape means. Finally he asked her outright whether her father forced her to have sex. In other words, did Trevor Jordache rape his younger daughter.

'No,' said Rachel in a loud, clear, firm voice. 'No. He didn't.'

Mandy and Beth's faces fell. The case for mitigating circumstances was blasted out of the water.

10th May 1995

Day three. We're all exhausted. Rachel can't have slept a wink. I met her several times on the way to the bathroom. We ended up drinking tea in the kitchen at 4am. Rachel just sat there, taking such small sips from her mug her lips weren't even wet. I couldn't get a word out of her. It was hardly the kind of situation where one could talk about the weather and I felt completely at sea broaching the main subject under consideration.

I wasn't sure if Rachel would want to go back to court, but she did. Now she had given evidence, she was allowed to sit in. It was the start of the case for the defence. Mr Anderson's speech was excellent. He spoke movingly of the hellish psychological strain Mandy and Beth were under – a classic case of diminished responsibility. I felt he should have played up the provocation angle – surely Trevor's constant beatings were obvious? But I learned from the usher chap at lunchtime that cumulative provocation was not allowed to be a defence in such a case.

Then Mandy took the stand. Mr Anderson going through her life with Trevor. The man was completely monstrous. Any tiny dereliction of duty – as he saw it - was enough to send him into a fury. He attacked her once because his shoes weren't polished highly enough. I fear she did not come across well. Her voice was so faint as to be almost inaudible and the tone was so flat the sound seemed to be coming from the wall. It was hard to believe the fear and desperation she described was real. The jury sat there impassively, taking it all in as though Mandy was describing a tea-party where one of the guests broke a cup. I wanted to shake each one of them till his (or her) teeth rattled.

The prosecutor, Tate, tore her apart ruthlessly. Mandy's blossoming friendship with Sinbad, which, God knows, was completely innocent, became a dastardly plot. This new pregnancy became further proof of her guilt, and it almost seemed for a while as if Sinbad were on trial. Although, I must say, considering his involvement, he's extremely lucky not to be.

More to the point was Mandy's vacillation in taking Trevor back in the first place. I must admit, it's hard to fathom that one out. How could she have trusted him when he'd behaved to utterly appallingly? And why didn't she contact the authorities when the violence began again? Mandy's only response was that she didn't know. Although on reflection I can actually start to understand. Even I was taken in by his act of reformation when I showed him where Mandy lived.

Then Mandy made an appalling blunder. After the bogus funeral, Brenna badgered Mandy for the return of a signet ring. Of course, it was not available as Trevor had been wearing it the night he died. Counsel for the prosecution wouldn't leave the point alone. Brenna had got it back, so where had it come from? Had Mandy had the presence of mind to take it from him as she pulled the knife from his back? Had she gone into the extension during the time Trevor was stinking out there? Why hadn't she given the ring to Brenna straight away?

Mandy reached the end of her tether.She blurted out that weeks after she and Beth had buried the body under the patio and put concrete flagstones over the grave, they'd disinterred the corpse to get the ring. An eerie silence fell upon the court.

Tate was merciless: 'You dug up the dead body of a man you stabbed in order to pull a signet ring off the putrefying flesh of his rotting hand. In order to pacify your sister-in-law.'

Mr Anderson and Alison Dicks made frantic signs to each other. It was obvious that this revelation was completely new to them. The prosecution's version of a manipulative, cold, evil woman suddenly seemed all too plausible. According to him, Mandy was hell bent on revenge because her husband had beaten her up a bit and, worse, wasn't as financially successful as he could have been.

I fear things are looking grim for Mandy and Beth. When we got back, Rachel locked herself in her bedroom. She wouldn't even come out for supper. Jean said it was best to leave her. She and I spent the evening going over and over the day's events. According to my good lady, Mandy was too terrified of Trevor and had been let down by the authorities too many times to seek help. After all, she'd come to a safe house, given to her by a charity specializing in helping battered wives, and still he'd managed to track her down.

I felt a stroke of guilt so strong I was almost overwhelmed. Once again, in my mind I saw Trevor Jordache, newly released from prison, enter the Close looking for Mandy. In my capacity as chairman of the B.R.A., I was only too helpful. I led him right to his victim. Not our place to interfere. None of our business. If only I'd alerted the police. Done something. But no. I crossed to the other side of the street like everyone else, so that the full tragedy could unfold.

11th May 1995

Beth took the stand today. I must admit that at first she put up a jolly good show. You could see how upset she was, tears were streaming down her face throughout the ordeal, yet she managed to speak up and tell her story simply and clearly.

The first sticky moment came when counsel for the defence questioned her about Rachel and the alleged abuse. It's all so circumstantial. Beth came home one night to find her mother lying on the floor. That animal had beaten her unconscious. In a panic, Beth leapt up the stairs to check on her sister, only to find her lying in bed with her father. He had his arms around her and the two of them were sleeping. Exactly as Rachel had described, only seen through Beth's eyes, the scene became terribly ominous. Beside me, Rachel sat absolutely rigid. She didn't move a muscle throughout Beth's cross-examination.

It was at that moment, faced with the proof of her father repeating the same terrible pattern, that Beth realized the only thing to do was to kill him.

'I couldn't feel anything at first,' she said. 'It was like my head was going to explode. I kept hearing this voice in my head saying Kill him! Kill him! Kill him! Kill him!'

'Is that what you wanted to do?' was Anderson's next question.

'No,' she replied. 'I just wanted Mum and Rachel to be safe. I wanted him out of our lives before he drove us all mad or killed us. I didn't know what I was doing or what I was thinking. There was this man living with these three women and he'd raped them all. Somebody, somehow had to do something about it.'

She didn't know what she was doing or what she was thinking. Was there ever a clearer case of diminished responsibility?

Mr Tate went on the attack immediately. If he said the word 'alleged' once, he said it a hundred times. Basically, he did everything he could to persuade the jury that the whole sorry history of sexual abuse – of Rachel AND of Beth – was completely fabricated. His voice rang out over the court room.

'You saw no rape. You heard no rape. Your own sister testifies that there was no rape.'

Instead, he presented a totally different version of events. According to him, Mandy wanted vengeance, so she poisoned her daughter's mind against her husband, as she was soon to poison his body. It was utterly ludicrous! Of course, there were no witnesses to the abuse. The man may have been a monster, but he was no fool. On the contrary, he was an insinuating, charming, plausible creature, who knew exactly where to find his victim's weak spot.

Then Beth made her fatal mistake – one even more telling than Mandy's startling revelation yesterday. The prosecution wanted to know what incident in particular made Trevor so furious that night. Weakened by the weedkiller as he was, why was he bludgeoning Beth with such force? At first, Beth said she couldn't remember, but the questions went on and on. Finally, there was an outburst.

'It was the tablets,' she shouted.

Again, I saw the look of utter consternation and amazement on the faces of the defence counsel and the solicitor. In the dock, Mandy went white.

Three times the prosecution counsel demanded to know what tablets she was referring to. Eventually, Beth caved in.

'The ones that I was crushing up to put in his hot milk because the weedkiller didn't work. We had to get rid of him. We didn't know what else to do. For God's sake, the man was a psychopath.'

Mr Tate sat down in triumph. It was a disaster for our side. How can any jury fail to convict having heard that not one, but two attempts at poisoning the man were made?

Beth looked dismayed at being dismissed. She refused to go and began a tirade against British justice.

'I want to know why we're on trial for protecting ourselves against that vicious beast. I want to know why he was never punished for what he did to us and why women end up in prison for life for trying to protect themselves from animals like my father. Against the scum who think that a wedding ring is a licence to terrorize, to punch and kick and hurt and rape.'

Of course, she was entirely right, but this was neither the time nor the place for a political speech. As she got shriller and more hysterical, I could feel any sympathy the jury had for her ebb away. She was presenting herself exactly as the prosecution wanted her to – the strident, lesbian man-hater.

12th May 1995

Another sleepless night. Jean and I went over and over what happened yesterday, sometimes hopeful, more often in despair. We heard Rachel sobbing her heart out. Jean knocked, but Rachel refused to open the door. She didn't say a word at breakfast.

After the alarms and diversions of yesterday, proceedings were relatively quiet. The defence called in witnesses to testify to Trevor's brutality. A Mrs Shackleton spoke on behalf of the battered women's refuge. In all her long years of experience of violent men, she said she had seldom seen injuries as brutal as those Trevor Jordache inflicted on his wife. He crossed the boundary into frenzy. It was a wonder Mandy wasn't killed herself.

A set of pictures of the injuries was passed around. Of course, we in the public gallery couldn't see them, but even the heartless Tate turned pale. At least one member of the jury had tears in her eyes. I glanced across at Rachel, still stony-faced and unmoving. Why is she so determinedly loyal to her father after what he did?

Sinbad was called up next as a witness for the defence. I must say I hardly recognized our local window-cleaner in his suit. He created a very good impression. The prosecution's extraordinary rigmarole of a man taken in by a calculating harpy sounded hollow when set against Sinbad's quiet, straightforward testimony.

After lunch came the summing up. The prosecution talked of a tale of unprecedented wickedness and evil. The defence focused on the women's total loss of self control. Mandy and Beth had been so tortured and abused that their distinction between reality and illusion was totally distorted. All rational principles that guide normal behaviour had dissolved. I only hope the jury agrees.

I thought the judge's summing up was extremely fair. In fact, he seemed to lean more heavily on the evidence for the defence than the prosecution. Mandy and Beth are pleading not guilty on the grounds of diminished responsibility and self-defence, but the judge told the jury there was another option. Manslaughter. If Mandy, faced with a violent attack on her daughter, coupled with her husband's verbal threats to kill them all, spontaneously lost all control, then she is guilty of the lesser crime. It was the last thought left with the jury before they retired. We'll have to wait until Monday now to hear the verdict. But I can't help believing or at least hoping, that the judge was offering some form of lifeline to Mandy and Beth.

14th May 1995

A strange weekend. All three of us – Jean, Rachel and myself – were in a sort of state of suspended animation. Merely waiting for Monday to come. Outwardly, we passed the time in a normal enough way. Breakfast, lunch, dinner - Saturday. Breakfast, lunch, dinner – today. Yet I can't for the life of me recall a single morsel that passed my lips.

Rachel has been completely quiet and withdrawn. Kept to her room most of the time. We tried the distraction of the Monopoly board, but none of us could concentrate. None of us gave a damn who had hotels on Mayfair. Even the lure of the scrabble board seemed to pale.

This evening, Rachel packed her bags. She's planning to go straight to Ireland with her Aunt Brenna after the verdict. I suppose she'll be better off with a member of her own family, but I can't help being concerned. Brenna's so bitter about Mandy and Beth, she's bound to make sure Rachel loses all contact with them.

I'm also sad to think that we'll probably never see her again ourselves. I've got so used to having her round the place. As horrific as these last few weeks have been and even though Rachel's been so upset and withdrawn, our lives have been enriched by her company. It'll be very hard to say goodbye.

15th May 1995

We were all back in court first thing for the verdict. The whole day felt unreal. Like a nightmare. I only wish there was a way to wake up.

Brenna Jordache caught up with us on the steps, then we ran into Mandy and Sinbad in the corridor where the details of the day's hearings are pinned up. Jean and I thought it tactful to make a strategic withdrawal to the cafeteria to give Rachel a chance to talk to her mother – and possibly to say goodbye.

The place was chock-a-block again. Crowds of sightseers and journalists fighting for the ground mud they have the cheek to label coffee. The facilities were woefully inadequate. I ought to complain, but I haven't the heart after what happened.

We returned to find a full-scale row had developed between the two sides of the family. Beth was calling her aunt an evil bitch. I was shocked and about to intervene when the truth came out. It was Brenna who had sent the hate mail and the death threats. So much for her pious evocations on behalf of her beloved brother. They were as bad as each other.

Poor Rachel was devastated. Of course it was absolutely impossible for her to go to Ireland under those circumstances. She elected to remain with Jean and myself, saying she wanted to stay with people who cared about her. Despite the tension, I felt a warm glow when she said that. Seems she'll be our guest, part of our family for the foreseeable future.

Mandy had given Rachel a letter to read in case the worst came to the worst. We found a relatively quiet spot, in a corner unsullied by press parasites. I don't know what was in it, but Rachel wept silently until we were called in for the verdict.

Guilty. Both of them. On all counts.

The judge, whom I'd thought was positively gunning for the defence, sentenced Mandy to life imprisonment and Beth to five years.

There was pandemonium when this was announced. After behaving so impeccably, Sinbad lost control.

'You can't do that,' he shouted at His so-called Honour. 'Are you deaf or something? Didn't you hear what she went through? You should be giving her compensation, not locking her up. Is this what you call justice?'

He had to be restrained by the officials. The judge ordered the prisoners to be taken down. Sinbad rushed up to the dock. He and Mandy clung to eachother until policemen and prison warders could prise them apart. She was dragged away as he promised over and over again that he'd wait for her.

How did it happen? What was the jury thinking about? How could they come to such a verdict? They completely ignored the appalling violence meted out by Trevor. And the judge gave them the opportunity to reduce the charge to manslaughter. Why didn't they take it, if they honestly couldn't accept the pleas of self-defence and diminished responsibility? This whole business has severely dented my belief in British justice.

16th May 1995

Today's headlines were gloating. COURT JAILS EVIL WOMEN. Evil women? Mandy and Beth? The miscarriage of justice makes me sick. It's breaking Sinbad's heart. He and Mick Johnson came round this afternoon to see if there's anything to be done.

The poor chap was utterly bewildered by the swiftness of events. Mandy and Beth were simply whisked away. Sinbad didn't get a chance to find out where they were being taken. He doesn't know how to write to them, let alone visit. All he had registered was the look of terror on Mandy's face when she had to go.

Presumably there'll be an appeal. And there will definitely be some kind of visiting rights. Also, we need to know precisely what 'life' means. Sinbad put his finger on the nub of the problem – how old will the baby be when Mandy is released. What's the rule about time off for good behaviour?

This is where an organization like the Brookside Residents' Association can really step in. We're holding a meeting tomorrow night *chez moi* to see what we can do. In the meantime, Mick Johnson has been deputized to help Sinbad ring the solicitor.

Rachel, unsurprisingly, kept to her room today. She was very quiet and extra-polite. I don't think the reality has sunk in yet. Jean and I have agreed that the best policy is to leave her to it for the moment, but to make sure she knows we're on hand if she needs us. There's not much more we can do for now.

17th May 1995

Spent the morning drumming up support for tonight's B.R.A. meeting. I was jolly glad to have something to do. Most people, I'm pleased to say, were only too willing to lend their wholehearted support.

There were one or two disappointments. Ron Dixon was damning. As far as he was concerned, our two were found guilty of murder and must therefore rot in jail. If he'd sat through the trial as I did, I'm sure he would have agreed that they were very harshly treated. Ron did point out that a life sentence could mean as little as eight years. We can only hope, but even so, eight years' incarceration is monstrously unfair.

I suppose I could have expected a less-than-generous attitude from Ron, but Max let me down completely. He agreed that the sentences were far too severe. His contention was that the B.R.A. was not in a position to do anything about it. I must confess to a feeling of great indignation. My son-in-law actually had the cheek to cast aspersions on our association. Our 'merry little band' as he described us may not be Amnesty

International, but I think he vastly underestimates what solid community spirit can achieve. It seems clear to me now why he failed to support our V.E. celebrations.

Rachel had to be told about the meeting, of course. I went up to her room with a spot of lunch and found her crying her eyes out. She's obviously been brooding on her mother and sister's terrible fate. By the time Beth is released, Rachel will be twenty. No longer a teenager. Beth will be twenty-five. What will that do to her studies? Rachel's main fear is that if Mandy has to stay behind bars for years, she'll forget what her youngest daughter looks like. I tried my best to comfort her, but those kinds of worries aren't done away with in an instant. They go too deep. I wish Jean had been there at that moment. I'm all at sea when it comes to the emotional bit.

Unsurprisingly, Rachel has elected to be absent while the meeting's on. I'll have to finish this entry here, as the kettle is boiling and the hoards will be descending any minute.

18th May 1995

We'll show Max. The Brookside Residents' Association will do its damnedest to secure the release of the Jordache Two. Sinbad, Rosie Banks, Mick Johnson and Patricia joined Jean and myself at the conference table.

Poor old Sinbad's still in a state of shock. He couldn't get through to Alison Dicks, as she was in court all day.

Until the matter can be discussed with her, the question of appeal remains unanswered.

Everyone was inclined to be extremely gloomy, so I thought it was about time for a bit of positive thinking. I proposed we put together a sub-committee to gather as much information as possible. Then we will be in a position to formulate a plan of action.

Patricia showed herself to be truly a chip off the old block. She volunteered straight away to chair. It's the perfect job for her with her PR background. We're bound to need some sort of publicity campaign. Rosie chipped in with an offer of help. In the end, we decided the sub-committee should consist of Patricia Farnham (chair), Rosie Banks, Jean Crosbie and Mick Johnson. I think such a formidable grouping should produce some results. We'll show Max Farnham what our merry little band can do.

Sinbad stayed behind after the meeting was over. He wanted a word with Rachel. She agreed to an interview in the garden, but to no avail. Sinbad reported that he'd asked her if she'd go to visit her mother once the system was sorted out. She refused. She's still far too angry about the whole business, not least the way she was dragged from pillar to post all over the Irish Republic. Sinbad again asked her to stay with him, at which point Rachel turned on her heel and went back into the house.

19th May 1995

I had the day to myself. Jean took Rachel for a day out to Blackpool to see the sights and do a bit of shopping. Take her mind off things for a bit.

To be honest, I was glad of the solitude. I spent the time pottering about. The Cortina was in need of urgent attention. I haven't had a minute to see to the old girl lately. It's quite a responsibility keeping a genuine classic on the road. Amazing to think she was being driven during the notorious sixties. I'd like to see one of these modern tin cans still on the road in thirty years' time.

I retired to my shed this afternoon, for a good CB session. A gratifying substantial number of regulars queried my absence from the airwaves and were only too interested to hear about the events that had separated me from my call sign. Nearly everyone I spoke to expressed disapproval of the verdict.

Sinbad and Mick called in on the way back from seeing Alison Dicks. They were in a sombre mood. Her news wasn't good. For a start, nothing's going to happen overnight. The appeals procedure could take months. First, the appeal has to be granted. Miss Dicks has registered an intention to appeal, but she hasn't yet had time to do any detailed work on the grounds. The snag is that we need new evidence. At the moment, there's no chance of the pair getting off on a technicality. The most they've got so far is an argument that the trial wasn't fair because of the publicity surrounding it. Even to my ears, that sounds pretty thin.

Jean and Rachel came home laden with shopping bags. Apparently, Rachel had been very depressed, although it was obvious she was making an effort to appear cheerful. It distressed Jean considerably. Over coffee, she told Rachel she need not hide her feelings with us. The result was a rather weepy session on the pier. By the time they got back, Rachel seemed a tad more relaxed. She's not smiling, of course, but at least it looks like there's a person living behind her face.

20th May 1995

The Jordache Campaign Sub-Committee this afternoon. I retreated to my shed, but Jean gave me chapter and verse afterwards. There has been a fresh blow. Alison Dicks telephoned Sinbad this morning to tell him that the Home Office has issued an official indication of how long Mandy will have to serve. The poor woman is to be imprisoned for a minimum of twelve years.

Twelve years! It's unbelievable. By the time she's released, her unborn child will be in secondary school. She can't be allowed to rot in gaol all that time.

The consternation felt by the entire sub-committee fuelled their brains. Alison Dicks said that keeping the case in the public eye may do some good, so that's the task shouldered by the Brookside Residents' Association. The first step is to get a petition together. Rosie works as a traffic warden, so she meets the public every day. Mick will have pages on the counter of the Pizza Parlour. Naturally, all of Sinbad's window-cleaning clients will sign.

Posters were the next item on the agenda. Patricia has a pet printer, who's prepared to run them off quickly and cheaply. Sinbad is to provide pictures. Luckily, he's got some excellent holiday snaps. Between us, we are in touch with a large number of shops where the posters can be displayed.

We're going to have to do more than that, however. Patricia still has contacts in the press. She's been detailed to get in contact with magazines, radio and television to try to get a debate going about women and violence. It's time to start making the media work for us. If our campaign's successful, Mandy and Beth will be out in time for the birth of Sinbad Junior.

22nd May 1995

There are definitely no flies on my Patsy. The posters have arrived already. And jolly good they look too. The pictures Sinbad found are splendid. No-one could believe that such innocent, normal women could possibly be cold-hearted killers. The banner headline above the photos reads MANDY AND BETH JORDACHE ARE INNOCENT. Underneath in large letters it says VICTIMS OF DOMESTIC VIOLENCE SHOULD NOT BE PUNISHED. WE NEED YOUR SUPPORT TO CHANGE THE LAW. WRITE TO YOUR LOCAL MP NOW AND FREE THE JORDACHE

WOMEN. SIGN OUR PETITION.

Just what we need. A good clear stark message. Jean was out on distribution patrol first thing. Mick put one up in the Pizza Parlour window and there's one in La Luz as well.

Sinbad went to visit Mandy and Beth for the first time today. Apparently, both of them looked awful. Didn't take long for the prison pallor to set in. Even the news about the campaign didn't cheer them up. I'm sure when we start to see results, they'll rally round.

Rachel continues to ignore the whole thing. Ostensibly, her entire attention is taken up with good old GCSEs. For the moment, Jean and I are playing along. Maybe she'll come out of her shell in due course. I was rather hoping to be able to be of some assistance with the revision, but I discovered that when it comes to the contemporary curriculum, I'm completely at sea. Information technology or IT is the worst. It hadn't even been invented in my time. Still, I always welcome an opportunity to expand my intellectual horizons and this is certainly a challenge.

24 May 1995

Had a bit of a brainwave today. It suddenly occurred to me that Rachel's great friend Lee Banks is a bit of a computer whizz kid. I popped over to see if there was any chance of a quick briefing on the subject. Lee himself wasn't about, but Rosie kindly rooted around in his room and came up with a couple of likely-looking tomes. They've proved to be just the ticket. I spent a most instructive afternoon boning up on them.

I have to say that Rachel's enthusiasm was less than boundless. In fact, she described IT as about as interesting as watching paint dry. Still, I think she appreciated the help.

Whilst Rachel and I were *tête-à-tête*, as it were, it seemed a good opportunity to broach the subject of Sinbad's visit to Mandy and Beth. He was very keen to talk to her about it. Unfortunately, she politely made it abundantly clear that she didn't want to know. I'm sure she must be seething inside, but all we get is a polite, quiet, totally remote response.

Sinbad himself came over to plead his case. As soon as he appeared, Rachel went AWOL. It's as though she can't even stand to be under the same roof as him. The poor man was really cut up by her reaction.

He had another reason for his visit. Mandy has authorized him to pay us for Rachel's keep. Naturally, Jean and I refused. It really is almost as cheap to feed three as two. Sinbad insisted, however, pointing out that providing a little cash will make Mandy feel she's still got a say in her daughter's care.

It occurred to me that perhaps we ought to make Rachel's residence a little more official. Use this address for school, medical records, passports and so on. Apart from anything else, it might make her feel she really belongs somewhere. Jean and I had already discussed it as the most sensible option.

Unfortunately, Sinbad took the suggestion badly. I wouldn't have thought Mandy would object, but he said it would break her heart. He won't even try to explain the plan to her.

27th May 1995

Sinbad may not have wanted to talk to Mandy about our scheme, but he had no scruples about telling Patricia. She came haring over to see us, guns a-blazing.

She thinks we're making a big mistake.

'In the final analysis,' she said. 'She's not your responsibility.'

Not our responsibility? Perhaps not in law, but morally she is, given the circumstances. I know Patricia only has our best interests at heart. As far as she's concerned, we're opening our retirement up to all sorts of problems. If only she lived with Rachel, she'd see how easy the whole thing is.

Besides, what would happen to her if we asked her to leave? As far as I can see, if she doesn't become a permanent fixture here, there are three alternatives.

1. She goes back to live with Sinbad – a move to which she is vehemently opposed.
2. Mandy gets released from prison and everyone lives happily ever after. A highly unlikely scenario.
3. The most probable outcome is that she ends up in some dingy bedsit, alone at sixteen years of age and

a prey to every low-life and sleazy character that happens along.

Jean and I will *not* abandon that girl.

30th May 1995

The campaign is forging ahead. A group called Women Against Violent Men have contacted Patricia. They've taken up Mandy and Beth's plight as one of their causes and are mounting a protest tomorrow night. It's to take the form of an all-night vigil on St. George's hall platform. The theme is men's violence towards women and our case is to be highlighted. Apparently, a large number of local women have already pledged to be there. Support amongst the neighbours has been really strong.

My task is somewhat on the sidelines – ensuring the flasks are well filled and the sandwiches are cut. It's a women-only event. To be honest, I'm not absolutely sorry. Once one is over sixty, the lure of a night on the pavement has distinctly lost its appeal. Jean, however, is raring to go. She's really taken this cause to heart. I must say I'm proud of her.

Her enthusiasm was fired even more by her visit to the prisoners today. She came back very quiet and shaken. The surroundings were pretty grim. After all, the place is a prison. It's not supposed to be comfortable and pleasant. Jean was supposed to be there to cheer Mandy and Beth up, but she ended up in tears herself, through sheer fright and frustration.

Rachel provided us with a tiny glimmer of hope. Despite the initial agreement to keep the prison visit quiet, Jean spilled the beans over the washing up. It was a propitious moment and the more open we can be with Rachel the better. Rachel declared herself 'not bothered' by the news, but there was a chink in the armour of her lack of interest. Jean mentioned that Mandy had inquired after her daughter. There was a long, long pause, then Rachel asked if they were OK. A simple question, but a momentous one. It's the first time she's shown the slightest concern for them. Jean suggested in the gentlest manner that a visit would do Mandy a great deal of good, but Rachel went straight back into her shell.

'I'm not bothered' is her standard response. Who does she think she's kidding?

1st June 1995

Jean and Patsy returned in triumph from the vigil last night. It was an enormous success. Hundreds of women, some from hundreds of miles away, turned up to lend their support. There were speakers and music and silent moments in the candlelight. A good time, in fact, was had by all. One of the speeches was specifically about the Jordache case. Jean reported that feelings on the matter ran very high, with a great many cheers for Beth and Mandy and boos for the authorities who incarcerated them.

This morning's paper carried an excellent photograph of the event. I was a tad disappointed not to be able to pick out Jean and Patsy, but it did give a good indication of the numbers involved.

Max is proving a slight fly in the ointment. He is less than keen on Patricia's activities. For one thing, he's worried about the Gift Box. They went to see the bank manager for a loan the other day and were unceremoniously turned down. With Barry still overseas, Max is running the restaurant single-handed. Obviously, the Gift Box must stay open to make money.

He's not going to convince anyone by these little digs and gibes he keeps making. Patricia has never responded well to being patronized. The more he decries her involvement, the more she'll dig her heels in. That's our Patsy.

This is, however, a patch of troubled water on which I can pour oil. Whilst Patsy is on campaign duty, I am prepared to serve behind the counter. Should be rather fun. The only problem is the gift-wrapping service. When it comes to ribbon curling, I'm all thumbs.

2nd June 1995

I've just read over yesterday's entries. After today's fiasco, I'm inclined to think Max might have a point.

First of all, there's the TV programme. A satellite company is doing a special on domestic violence feature next week. It's one of those early-morning debating affairs called 'Loud and Clear'. Never seen it myself as I wouldn't be caught dead with one of those appalling dish affairs defiling my walls. However, they seem to have quite a following. Patricia contacted them and they invited a couple of campaigners to be part of the panel.

Without wishing to blow my own trumpet, I would have thought as chairman of the B.R.A. I was the natural choice. Besides, I watch *Question Time* every week. But no. Apparently, if I want to appear I'll have to have a sex change. It's another women-only event. This is all getting to be rather sexist.

In fact, the whole thing is getting out of hand. Jean and I were on Gift Box duty this afternoon. Things were horribly quiet, so Jean slipped off with Sinbad for an hour or so. She was distinctly evasive about what they were up to. When they hadn't returned four hours later, I was very worried. So was Mick Johnson, who'd lent Sinbad the Pizza Parlour's delivery van. He had a number of hungry and irate customers in desperation for their Margheritas.

I was about to telephone the authorities, when a police car drew up in full view of the entire Parade. Jean stepped out, cool as a cucumber, wearing the most ridiculous tee-shirt affair over her frock. It was emblazoned with a replica of the Jordache campaign poster. The sentiments may have been admirable, but the garment itself was rather unbecoming on a person of Jean's age.

'I've been arrested for flyposting,' she proudly announced to the world.

The ignominy of it! The wife of the chairman of the Brookside Residents' Association escorted home by the local constabulary. Was she even remotely remorseful? No. She was positively proud of herself. The woman had absolutely no consideration for my position and the embarrassment her appalling behaviour would cause me. Ron Dixon was laughing his head off.

I will not have her resorting to criminal means. I insisted that she discuss her strategy with me before she went on campaigning. To be frank, she gave me the raspberry.

'I'll do no such thing,' she said. 'I happen to be my own person.'

This is all going too far.

5th June 1995

A quiet weekend on the whole. Rachel kept to her room most of the time. I do wish she'd come out of her shell a bit. She spent Saturday night with Lee Banks. He's basically a nice lad. I can't see them getting up to too much mischief. Rachel was back well before 10pm.

On Sunday evening, I managed to lure her out with the promise of beating me into a cocked hat at Scrabble. Jean was next door at Patricia's planning their strategy for the TV show, so Rachel and I had a cosy evening to ourselves. I was careful that the words 'mother', 'prison' and 'Sinbad' didn't appear on the board.

The campaign has got completely out of hand. Jean

was helping out at the Gift Box. Around half past three, I thought a spot of Earl Grey tea was in order, so I went round there to proffer the cup that cheers. When I opened the door, I was greeted by a gale of cackling, drunken merriment. It was unbelievable. Patricia was in pride of place atop the counter, laughing uncontrollably. Jean was just as bad. Positively rolling around the place. They were being egged on by Jackie Corkhill and young Beverley. The entire scene was utterly disgraceful. In centre stage was an enormous and empty bottle of champagne. It turned out later to have been a misguided present from that oaf Jimmy Corkhill to his long-suffering wife.

I really thought Jean would have had more sense. Her breath positively reeked of alcohol. All I can think is that her hormones are playing up. I fear next we'll have all that lesbian nonsense dragged up again. I took her away at once, but she was totally unrepentant. She's in the bedroom now, sleeping it off. And this is the woman who thinks she's a suitable candidate to represent the Brookside Residents' Association on national television tomorrow!

6th June 1995

Despite the alarms and diversions, the show went off remarkably well. Patricia and Jean set off for the studio first thing. Once they'd gone, I realized there was a slight snag. No satellite. The only people in the Close who have succumbed to that particular iniquity are the Dixons and the Banks. Rosie wasn't in, so I popped next door, cap in hand, to beg a place in front of the box at Casa Bevron. I collided with Max on the doorstep, who'd registered the same problem and come up with the same solution.

There really was absolutely no need for Beverley to be quite so triumphant. Admittedly, Max can be a touch snobbish at times and there has been growing rivalry between the two households re good taste and electronic gadgetry. However, at times like these, it's up to neighbours to pull together and set aside their differences. Luckily, Beverley did so just in time for the programme to start.

The first shock was that Jean wasn't on the panel after all. She told me afterwards that when she was actually faced with talking on live TV, she lost her bottle, to use the vernacular. Instead, there was Jackie Corkhill sitting next to Patricia. Michael Parkinson was in the chair, so I knew we were in for a good debate.

Facing the two ladies was an undesirable type known as Ronnie, who claimed that his violence against women was a result of reading and watching violent material in the media. This must by now be a truism. It's perfectly obvious that the increasing nudity and bad language perpetuated before and after the watershed must take its share of the blame for the disgraceful decline in standards. Next to him sat a rather pompous-looking young man, James something, MP for somewhere or other.

Mr Parkinson turned first to Patricia. She did splendidly. Put her case clearly and concisely, saying that the laws concerning domestic violence should be changed.

'The law as it stands only allows women to use "reasonable force" when defending themselves against attack by a violent partner,' she said. I'd heard her rehearsing this speech with Jean. 'A woman in that situation is then treated by the courts as the aggressor.'

Of course, you can't expect an experienced presenter like Michael Parkinson to give anyone an easy ride.

'Are you suggesting that women should be allowed to use unreasonable force?' he countered.

'No. What we're saying is that a woman who is constantly and systematically abused should be able to defend herself and her children by whatever means necessary.'

Does that include murder?

Patricia pointed out that killing under such circumstances shouldn't necessarily always be regarded as murder. Certainly not in the same way as a mugger who kills or a serial killer. The Jordaches are two innocent women who were physically and sexually abused over a number of years.

I thought her next speech was very moving. 'They are the real victims,' she said. 'But they're still suffering. They're locked away in a jail because they defended themselves.'

'But what they did was very wrong,' was Parkie's next riposte. 'You can't escape that. They murdered someone. They took the law into their own hands.'

'They had no choice. They did what any woman in their position would have done.'

'Any woman? Are you saying you would do the same thing in their situation? You would use any kind of force to defend yourself?'

That really put Patricia on the spot. In the heat of the moment, she got rather carried away.

'I suppose so. I'd do anything to protect myself and my children from an abuser.'

'Would that include killing your own husband?' There was a pause as the impact of this last question sank in.

Patricia's voice was very quiet as she answered. 'If he was abusing me? Yes. I would kill him. I'd kill my own husband.'

At this, Max positively exploded with rage. I was so involved in what was happening on screen, I'd completely forgotten my companions. He vented his anger by switching the television off. Most annoying as the rest of us were still glued.

Sometimes, I truly regret Patsy's decision to marry him. He was utterly ridiculous, accusing my daughter of making him out to be the same kind of monster as Trevor Jordache. As if she would! She was merely making a point in an emphatic manner. His statement that she would have to choose between him and the campaign was melodrama, pure and simple. If he goes on like this it won't be much of a choice.

Beverley switched the TV back on, but we still missed several precious moments. Michael Parkinson had gone on to question the MP. A smooth individual if ever I saw one, totally unconcerned with the plight of women today. In his eyes, the law is correct and unquestionable. Never mind the subject fear borne by millions of wives, daughters and girlfriends. A terror so overwhelming they daren't go to the police or social services.

My hackles were rising – and so it seems were Jackie Corkhill's. Up until then, she hadn't said a word, although the camera panned back to her disgusted expression on several occasions. But the MP was too much for her. She launched into a tirade of pure scouse. It was truly impressive. Combined with Patricia's well-prepared and thoughtful arguments, her gut reactions had the audience applauding, even cheering by the end of it.

'The Jordache women were tortured and abused for nearly twenty years,' she burst out. 'No law, no MP, nobody did anything to protect them. Those women had to look out for themselves because they were left to it. They were let down by this society. Swept under the carpet. You just lock them up and want to throw away the key. You don't know what this country's really like. Those two women should have got medals for what they did, not prison sentences. I'll tell you what, mate, the law's not working. And you're not working either. You're a waste of space and a waste of taxpayers' money.'

Which just about says it all for politicians.

13th June 1995

Damn the media! When their intrusion will only make matters worse, the bloodsuckers stick to your skin like leeches. When there's a legitimate cause to publicize, they're nowhere to be seen.

The Jordache Two have sunk without trace. Despite Patricia's tireless efforts, there's been no new coverage for over a week. How are we going to get them released at this rate?

The only event on the horizon is the petition. Several thousand people have signed and it makes a pretty impressive bundle of paper. Patsy was detailed to draft a letter to go with it. Naturally, she enlisted my help. Letter-writing has always been my forte. We spent a pleasant afternoon getting it exactly right. I'm jolly glad I was around to help. Patricia is a product of our degenerate modern age. She was most reluctant to couch this official document in the appropriate language. How can we hope to impress John Major if we put 'don't' instead of 'do not'? It took me an hour's solid remonstration to get her to change it. That girl is stubborn. Gets it from her mother.

Sinbad had some worrying news. Alison Dicks had been in touch with him to say the police have released Trevor Jordache's body. His sister is burying him tomorrow. It's unbelievably short notice. I suspect nefarious dealings. Brenna must have known about this for some time. She really ought to have kept the interested parties informed.

As grim as the whole situation may be, it was my duty to tell Rachel. She has a right to know about her own father's funeral. Besides, this is exactly the kind of shock horror event the media are bound to home in on.

Rachel was predictably upset and angry when I told her, demanding to know why she hadn't been told before or asked what she wanted. My heart went out to her. The poor girl must feel utterly let down and betrayed. Sinbad spilt the beans as soon as he could, but her aunt has really let her down. This from the woman who was offering her a permanent home only a couple of weeks ago.

The upshot was that Rachel became determined to attend.

'I don't care if they've flown his body off to Australia,' she said. 'I'm going to be there.'

What could I do? In the end, I not only pledged to put up the money for the tickets, but to go with her. We dashed down to the travel agent's straight away. We leave from Speke at ten-thirty tomorrow morning.

14th June 1995

The funeral's come and gone, but we weren't there. At the last minute, as Rachel and I were literally getting into the cab to go to the airport, she changed her mind. It was obvious she'd spent the entire night thinking about it. Her face was drained of colour and her eyes were violet with exhaustion. Jean and I comforted her as best we could. Neither of us was about to force her to go.

Very calmly and sadly, she gave us an explanation. 'The more I thought about it, the more I couldn't face it. I've already said my goodbyes to him in my head anyway. I know it wasn't really my Dad in that coffin, but I didn't know that at the time. I believed it was him. I cried for him when I watched them bury him and I realized I'd never see him again. I don't need to go through all that again.'

It was as if she'd suddenly become an adult.

In an effort to bring some comfort, Jean pointed out that Rachel could go to any church and say a prayer in remembrance of her father. Rachel was keen on the idea and asked Jean to accompany her. Of course, she agreed, but I fear it was something of an ordeal. I regret to say that Jean is an agnostic.

It must have done some good. Rachel went to bed early and appears to have gone to sleep. Her light's off and there is no sound of sobbing. Jean told me that in the church Rachel seemed to regress back to vulnerable little girl. They discussed heaven in the simplest of terms – a problem for Jean who doesn't believe in it. Rachel's reason for rejecting it was the impossibility of reconciling the warring factions of her family. How could her father, mother, sister and aunt possibly get on in heaven when they disagreed with such tragic results in life? If there really is a God, why does he let such terrible things happen? Perhaps that is the oldest and most unanswerable mystery in the universe.

Jean took the opportunity to try to get Rachel to

understand what drove Mandy and Beth to do what they did. The poor girl is torn apart by it all. She is finally starting to admit that the way her father treated her mother was wrong, but her loyalties are still with her father. In her eyes, he always treated her well and loved her, which is more than she believes her mother does.

15th June 1995

Rachel is definitely coming out of her shell. I think the fiasco over the funeral affected her deeply. There's something important on her mind. She almost confided in Jean today, but backed off at the last minute. They were working happily together in the Gift Box when the conversation turned to Jean's childhood. It was so different to Rachel's. Jean was an only child, with loving, normal parents. She was definitely a daddy's girl. I vividly recall the tears in his eyes as he gave away his 'little treasure' on our wedding day.

In passing, Jean mentioned that she 'never went short of hugs'. Rachel picked up on that immediately, questioning her closely on exactly what she meant. What did these hugs consist of? Was there anything else? Any other contact?

As casually as she could, Jean asked if Trevor had ever shown affection apart from goodnight kisses. She said the reaction was like a door slamming shut. Suddenly, Rachel once again became the snappy, bolshy teenager resenting interference. Totally indignant at the mere suggestion that her father acted in any way wrongly.

What went on between them? What did that monster do to her? And how are we ever to get her to confide in us?

17th June 1995

I had a very similar conversation with Rachel today. I found her sobbing her heart out in her bedroom.

'It's like I'm being punished,' she wailed. 'I didn't ask for any of this to happen. I haven't done anything wrong. At least, I don't think I have.'

This last bit really made me sit up. It transpires that Rachel is feeling as though it's her fault Mandy and Beth are in prison. There is a certain warped logic to it – if they acted as they did to protect her, then she must take responsibility for her father's death. I did my best to reassure her that she carries no blame whatsoever for what happened.

Once she calmed down, Rachel started to question me closely about my relationship with Jean and Patricia. Had I ever hit them? Did I cuddle Patsy when she was little? I answered as honestly as I could. I told her I used to hug my daughter all the time. She was such an affectionate child and it was a natural way for me to show how much I loved and cared for her.

'So why do people keep telling me that what my Dad did to me was so wrong?' Rachel asked.

I decided this was the moment to bite the bullet. 'I

don't know what he did,' I replied carefully. 'Was it more than just cuddling?'

'It wasn't like Beth made it sound. He was never violent with me. But sometimes he used to . . .'

She got no further, breaking down completely. I put my arms round her while she wept uncontrollably. When I next looked up, Jean was standing in the doorway, a worried look on her face.

We discussed the matter in whispers in the lounge. Jean thought I was unwise to be alone with Rachel in her bedroom. People might get the wrong idea. What is society coming to when a man can't even offer a young girl some comfort without the finger of suspicion being pointed?

I'm sure Rachel was trying to tell me what Trevor used to do to her, couldn't bring herself to use the words. What sort of a man could abuse his own daughter like that? She was just an innocent child. She still is.

One thing is now very clear – Rachel lied to the court. The important thing now is for Jean and myself to keep her trust. Let her open up in her own time. This is only the beginning. If she does admit the truth, it could really swing it for Mandy and Beth. It could change everything.

19th June 1995

It's so frustrating! Rachel seems to have clammed up again. We've spent two solid evenings together, but she just keeps her eyes glued to the television. The atmosphere in the lounge is charged with things unsaid. I must admit I have used the old CB as an excuse to take a break from it.

Jean is going to see Mandy on Friday. We've agreed that she won't say anything about Rachel's half-revelations. The matter's so delicate and we don't want to raise any false hopes. If only we knew for sure what was going through Rachel's mind. It's the same for Sinbad. Letting him in on the secret will only add to his burdens. Besides, he'd be bound to tell Mandy and Beth.

The situation is desperate. Without any sort of fresh evidence, the appeal is unlikely to be successful. Alison Dicks is not optimistic about their chances at the moment. All we can do is wait and hope.

The campaign has hit a bit of a low spot. We've had a formal acknowledgment of our petition from the Home Office. It was only a standard letter, of course, but it's something to tell the papers. Apart from that, there's nothing planned whatsoever. The sub-committee is meeting tomorrow night chez nous. I feel I ought to be there. We've got to keep the momentum going.

20th June 1995

I know we're supposed to be gaining publicity by whatever means necessary, but this latest idea is going a bit too far. A sponsored darts marathon indeed! Have they no dignity?

It was Jackie Corkhill's idea. I must admit she's certainly putting her heart and soul into the campaign. She, Jean, Patricia and Rosie are planning to play all day and night, to see how long they can last. Rosie runs a pub team, so she'll have a word with the manager. No doubt he'll be delighted at the publicity and the additional custom. She also knows a large number of female darts enthusiasts, who may be persuaded to lend their support. Any money not needed for campaign funds will be donated to the battered wives charity that supported Mandy.

I suppose, in principle, it could attract attention, but the whole thing's going off half-cocked. The event is timetabled for tomorrow night, leaving us no time at all for preparation.

As for the men, we've been firmly relegated to the back room. Max is babysitting and I have been appointed official refreshments manager. I'm sure I'd be far more use in charge of press liaison. However, a democratic vote was held and, apart from my own dissension, the result was unanimous. Tomorrow night I can look forward to filling thermos flasks, cutting sandwiches and baking sausage rolls.

The meeting ended on a rather awkward note. Jackie Corkhill vented her feelings re Trevor Jordache with some vigour. Not one of us disagreed, but unfortunately Rachel overheard her. She burst into the room in a towering rage.

'How do you know what he was like?' she screamed. 'You didn't even know him. I don't know why you're all doing this. Me Mum was found guilty. How can you let people say these things?'

Jackie was mortified, but it has to be said she was only voicing the opinion of the rest of us. I couldn't coax Rachel out of her room again. God only knows how much this has set her back. Just as she seemed to be on the point of telling us something.

22nd June 1995

It's hard to say whether the darts marathon was a success or not. There was a very respectable number of participants. The sight of twenty or so ladies aiming for the bullseye was pretty impressive. And they lasted from eight at night to eight o'clock this morning.

Patricia arranged for the hacks from the local rags to attend. They took a quick group snap, accepted quantities of alcohol and disappeared rapidly. Sinbad brought the early editions to the pub as we were clearing up. One photo in the most insignificant freesheet, with around fifty fatuous words. Complete silence from the rest of the fourth estate. You would have thought a major event like this would have interested the *Guardian* at least. It's so typical. The moment the body was found, they camped out on our doorsteps for weeks. Yet when their co-operation could be helpful, they don't want to know.

I had a couple of rather unnerving encounters. As I was returning with the third round of replenished thermos flasks, I bumped into Max bundling Thomas and

Alice into the car. He is not a happy man. His day is quite hectic enough without the added burden of getting the children off. Patricia was totally unsympathetic when I reported back. As far as she's concerned, it's simply a good object lesson for him on the trials and tribulations of being a working mother.

More disturbing was an incident last night. The initial supplies of sandwiches ran out much quicker than expected, so I popped home for some more. I found Rachel in the living room, surrounded by a pile of letters. She was so involved in reading them, she didn't hear me come in.

I made a joke about them being love letters and she flew at me.

'They're private,' she snapped. In an instant, she'd whisked every letter out of sight and shut herself in her bedroom again.

Five minutes later, she was in the kitchen apologizing. I told her there was no need. She's entitled to her privacy after all, and I must have made her jump. The odd thing was that she went out of her way to emphasize that the letters were just personal trivia.

I've never seen her like that, so jumpy and bad-tempered. She obviously didn't want me to see those letters. I wonder what's in them that's so important.

23rd June 1995

I'm shaking all over. Jean got herself arrested for fly posting barely three weeks ago, now I've had to rescue her from prison. She and Jackie Corkhill went to see Mandy and Beth. All went smoothly until visiting time was over. Jackie then produced some of those strong plastic strips used to tie parcels when you *don't* want them coming loose. She proceeded to handcuff herself and Jean to Mandy and Beth.

The first I heard of the matter was when I received an urgent telephone call from the police. I leapt into the Cortina, only to find the electrics have gone. In desperation, I dashed to the Parade, just in time to see Jimmy Corkhill getting into the last minicab in sight. We ended up sharing, as it turned out he'd had a similar call.

We got to the prison gates to find Jean and Jackie still tied at the wrists, shouting 'FREE THE JORDACHE TWO' at the tops of their voices. The bloody press were already there, photographing the pair of them. I've never been so ashamed in my life. My wife making a total exhibition of herself in front of a jailbird like Corkhill. I'm right with her on this campaign, but there are limits. At this rate, she'll end up inside herself.

Jean was unrepentant. She actually had the nerve to complain because I didn't boast of her antics to the reporters as the wretched Jimmy did. As far as she's concerned, anything that attracts publicity is fair game. I dread to think what she'll come up with next.

25th June 1995

How could I have been so stupid? I was looking for some photographs of our last New Year's party. Jean suggested the drawer in Rachel's room. They weren't there, but on the bed lay a familiar-looking folder, emblazoned with cutouts of pop stars and with a fierce message on the front. THE SECRETS OF RACHEL J. KEEP OUT. Spilling out of it were the very letters Rachel had got so angry about the other day.

Why didn't I obey the instructions? Why didn't I just find the photos and close the door behind me? My curiosity got the better of me, especially when I realized a number of them had been written on prison note paper. I picked one up and started to read it.

'My darling Rachel,' it started. 'I'm missing you so much. You must promise not to tell anyone our little secret. Especially not Mum and Beth. They wouldn't understand.'

It was inevitable, I suppose. Rachel caught me in the act and flew off the handle, accusing me of sneaking through her things and spying on her. They're all she's got left of her dad.

Jean was equally furious. But I could hardly avoid the letters. They were lying all over the bed. Why is she so secretive? What on earth is she trying to hide? The trouble is, it's going to be a darned sight harder to find out now.

26th June 1995

I'm in a terrible dilemma. It's torture. Under normal circumstances, I'd never dream of reading anyone's private correspondence. Especially someone like Rachel, who is not only our guest, but under our protection. Her trust in us has already been shaken by last night's incident. It will be totally destroyed if she finds out I've been investigating her private affairs again.

On the other hand, these letters could be the key to the truth. They could even make the difference between Mandy and Beth walking free or spending most of the rest of their lives in prison.

Much as my conscience pricked, I felt I had to do something. The frustration was intolerable. Rachel went into town with the young Banks lad and Jean was at the Gift Box. I took advantage of having an empty house to do a little detective work. They weren't anywhere to be found in Rachel's bedroom. Presumably she moved them after our contretemps. I hunted everywhere I could think of, even my own potting shed, but they were nowhere to be found.

Jean's efforts have been taking quite a different direction. Far from being abashed at being displayed in front of a prison by every newspaper in the land, she's been positively encouraged. She, Jackie Corkhill and Rosie Banks are planning to stage a continuous protest outside the jail. It was Jackie's idea. Hardly surprising after her outspoken television appearance. I don't blame her for her enthusiasm, but they must surely remain within the bounds of decency and the law.

I found the three of them with Patricia in the Gift Box becoming highly excitable at the thought of sleeping bags and spirit stoves. As usual, the planning stage is being skimped. The notion was only mooted this morning, yet they plan to be entrenched by tonight. The whole thing's bizarre. Grown women camping out on the pavement. It smacks far too much of Greenham Common harpies for my liking. I'm surprised respectable women like Rosie Banks, not to mention my own wife and daughter, can even countenance it.

Max was furious. Unfortunately, his reaction was to wax sarcastic. Even I could have told him that wouldn't wash with Patricia. She was distinctly wavering when she realized it would mean being away from Thomas and Alice, but Max's comments really put her back up. The idiot told her she was getting carried away and that she should have got over the protesting phase after university. After that, Patricia pledged to be with them for as long as necessary.

None of them considered who is to look after the Gift Box whilst Patricia and Jean are doing their bit for women's rights. Jean accused me of creating complications. At least, they've agreed to work out some kind of rota. I dare say I'll be asked to step in and use my organizational skills when they realize it's simply not as easy as all that. For one thing, they have made absolutely no provision for lavatory facilities. I did not appreciate Jean's flippant remark that they could go behind a bush. Quite apart from anything else, there's nothing in the way of greenery within a mile of the prison. The whole thing gets more undignified by the minute.

Needless to say, Rachel was less than delighted when she found out. She got very hot under the collar, shouting and screaming in a way that's most unlike her. As far as she's concerned, Mandy and Beth are guilty and she doesn't understand why everyone's wasting their time on them. Especially Beth, for whom she reserves her fiercest anger. Worst of all, she now sees Jean as a traitor – going over to the other side, as it were. Jean did her best to calm her down, trying to get her to see that Beth hated Trevor for a reason, but I doubt if Rachel was listening.

28th June 1995

I have to confess this vigil affair is really taking off. Several women's groups have sent representatives. There must be thirty women there at least. They were on the television last night and it was, thank goodness, referred to as a peaceful and legitimate protest. In fact, I was quite proud of Jean. Rachel walked out of the room as soon as the item came on the news, slamming the door so hard the house shook.

Rachel gets more and more moody every day. It's as if the polite, honeymoon phase of her stay with us is over. The mask is starting to crack and the bewilderment and upset is beginning to show. I'd asked her to give me a hand in the Gift Box this afternoon, as the place is getting pretty busy. No sooner had she arrived than she got into a complete panic. She'd left her bag on the bus and dashed off to search for it before I could stop her.

Less than half an hour later, Rosie Banks came in bearing the lost property. A fellow passenger had returned it. She'd found the address from one of the letters in the bag! So that's where they were. Rachel must have decided to keep them on her at all times.

I checked to see that Rachel's purse and make-up were still there. Nothing missing, not even the cash. It's nice to know there are still some honest people around. I fear the same cannot be said about yours truly. The temptation of having the letters in my hand and knowing that Rachel would be away for some time was too much. The first few I read seemed innocent enough, then I came across one that took my breath away. It wasn't on prison paper and was dated fairly recently, so I would guess he wrote it when he found his family at number 10.

My dearest sweetheart Rachel,

I can't stop thinking about you so I thought I should put pen to paper again. It's difficult to say all the things I want to face to face. It's so important that you never mention these letters to anybody. It would spoil everything. All those special secret times we share. Nobody would understand how special they are to us. Especially Beth. You know how jealous she is of us. If she knew me and you were so close, she'd just fly off the handle and try and turn your Mum against me all over again.

I just want you to know how much I love you. You're the only one who keeps me sane and understands how I feel. I wish you could be here now to cuddle up to me and keep me warm under the covers. Remember, you must keep our little secret. You know how Beth would twist everything if she found out. She'd try to make out what we're doing is wrong, but it isn't. You know that, don't you? I can't wait for the next time we can spend some time by ourselves.

Lots and lots of love and kisses and hugs as always,

Dad

It practically spells out what was going on. The phrases speak for themselves – 'our little secret', 'Beth wouldn't understand', 'she'd try to make out what we're doing is wrong'. Of course she would! It doesn't take a genius to work out what that man was up to. There were lots of other letters in the same vein.

I was left sweating and trembling. That poor girl! What she's been through. The whole thing's totally horrendous. Unfortunately, the dilemma's worse than ever.

Jean and I spent hours talking over the matter. She disagrees that the letters are enough. The court could read them as simply the natural affection of a father towards his daughter. She's right that nothing's absolutely explicit. It's all hidden between the lines.

We've got to say something but what? 'By the way, Rachel, we happened to be going through your things and came across one of your father's letters.' She'd run a mile. But we're talking about evidence that could be crucial for an appeal. We can't just ignore it.

1st July 1995

I popped in on the vigil this afternoon. There must have been a hundred women there. Some treat the event as a day out, picnicking on the pavement and having a good old singsong. A fair number are going the whole hog and staying out at night. Jean is one of the latter, although I must say she seems to juggle sisterly solidarity with the needs of hearth and home.

Patricia was, frankly, less successful on that front. Max has been looking more and more distracted over the past few days and the children were becoming distinctly unkempt. Patricia finally came back to the shop today, a look of triumph on her face. Max had visited her on the front line, as it were, to beg her to come home. He'd actually admitted that all this sarcasm and patronage were simply to disguise the fact that he can't cope with managing the children and a full-time job. How he expects my Patsy to do just that, I don't know, but she agreed to give the protesting a rest.

I've been giving a lot of thought to the question of Rachel's letters. Now that I know they exist, I am surely duty bound to make Sinbad aware of them. Here is a piece of vital evidence, right under our noses. The burden of society is proving intolerable. Surely he has a right to know. It's the decent thing to do. As for

Rachel, I'm sure if we explained properly, she'd understand.

Blowing the gaff is going to have to wait a while, however. I called round to number 10 this evening, only to discover the bird has flown. Sinbad has decamped with Mick Johnson and his children to spend a week in a caravan by the seaside. The poor chap certainly deserves a bit of a break.

The only alternative is to take the letters to Alison Dicks, the solicitor. Jean vetoed the idea vehemently. Her argument is that Rachel might react extremely badly to us bulldozing our way into her bedroom to seize the evidence. The letters alone might not be enough. They're all allusion and innuendo. So we're back to playing a waiting game, holding our breaths until Rachel trusts us enough to open up. Meanwhile, those two women are left to rot in that godforsaken hole.

4th July 1995

The protest could be getting out of hand. A large number of police officers have appeared, complete with helmets, riot shields and fearsome-looking batons. I assumed they must be on a training exercise. There was no sign of trouble. Admittedly, the numbers have been growing every day, but everyone was simply sitting or standing in an orderly fashion on the pavement. Every so often, someone started a slogan-chanting session but that hardly constitutes a disturbance.

Apparently, the inspector in charge of maintaining public order on the prison's pavement had a word with Jean, Patricia and Jackie Corkhill about the arrival of potential troublemakers. It seems there's a bunch of anarchists and hooligans who will attach themselves to any protest, simply in order to cause trouble.

I insisted that the whole thing was called off straight away, but my words of wisdom went unheeded. Jean refused to leave. She's staying until Mandy and Beth are released and will not leave a second before.

As we stood discussing the matter, a couple of broken down old vans showed up. I did not like the look of the ruffians that poured out. A bunch of long-haired layabouts, whose clothes hadn't seen a washing machine in several months at least. They'd even brought their children. What sort of an example is that? We should be teaching our youngsters respect for the law, not introducing them to anarchy. As usual, my perfectly legitimate anxieties were brushed aside. Anyone can go and protest, as long as they're supporting Mandy and Beth and are behaving themselves. I hung around for a couple of hours in case of emergency, but it all seemed peaceful enough.

6th July 1995

It was Mandy's birthday today. Jean was due to visit her as Sinbad's away. To her utter delight, Rachel asked her to deliver a card. She's really making progress. Even better, she agreed to go along to wish her mother happy birthday in person.

When they got to the prison gates, there was a positive riot going on. Rent-a-mob had sent droves of disreputables to turn the vigil from a peaceful protest to violent anarchy. God knows where they came from. Despite calls from the authorities to co-operate, they refused to leave access for supply vehicles. The police took action immediately. Hundreds of officers swooped down on the crowd. Jean actually saw fights breaking out between officers and members of the public. Naturally, she hustled Rachel away as soon as possible.

It could well be that they'd got wind that something was up. Certainly the press had turned up in force. I watched the whole event on the news. In the midst of the trouble, the gates swung open and a white van emerged. Inside were Mandy and Beth. The authorities had taken notice of the protest alright. They'd decided to transfer the Jordache Two out of harm's way. You could see the anger in the crowd rising, even on the small screen. They positively mobbed the van. Even with the police being armed and practically outnumbering the protesters, it took a considerable amount of force to free it.

A number of arrests were made, including Jackie Corkhill and Rosie Banks. I consider that most unfair. They were perfectly innocent. Totally different from the wasters jumping on the nearest bandwagon. Besides, Rosie Banks is, I believe, pregnant. Although, I must say

I find it odd that her husband Eddie allowed her to attend the protest in that condition in the first place.

7th July 1995

Just because you lose a battle doesn't mean you lose the war. The protest is over, thank God, but the campaign will continue. I've had to spend the day rallying the troops. Jean, Jackie and Patricia have all sunk into the depths of despair.

Their mood wasn't lifted by the news of Mandy and Beth's whereabouts. The authorities have obviously given the matter a great deal of thought – make visiting as awkward as possible. They've been transferred to the middle of nowhere, right in the heart of the Yorkshire moors. The round trip will be a good four hours by car. God knows how you get there by public transport. Poor Sinbad's going to be devastated when he gets back. And what chance do we have of persuading Rachel to visit Mandy now?

My morale-boosting efforts were less than successful. The atmosphere of gloom permeated not only the bungalow, but the Close and the Parade. Even Jackie Corkhill was too depressed to come up with another madcap publicity stunt.

10th July 1995

Made rather a boo-boo this morning. A little bird whispered into my ear that Mick Johnson was thinking of tying the nuptial knot. Apparently, he's rather fallen for one of the teachers at his son's school. Unfortunately, my congratulations appear to have been a little premature. Mick positively barked at me and told me in no uncertain terms to mind my own business. I'll have to have a word with that little bird.

Sinbad has returned and came to see me. It was a very delicate interview. He was naturally delighted to hear about the letters. Almost too delighted. It was all I could do to stop him marching straight into Rachel's bedroom and grabbing the proof.

All he's interested in is getting Mandy and Beth out of prison. Rachel's welfare and her relationship with the family falls distinctly into second place. Sinbad actually said that if it came to a choice between the baby being born out of prison or Rachel never speaking to any of them again, he'd choose the baby every time.

If only he'll let us bide our time, he may not have to make that choice. We've got to bide our time. Rachel may well volunteer the truth in due course.

The best I could do was to persuade him to agree to hang fire for a few days. After that, he'll get them by fair means or foul and hand them over to the solicitor.

12th July 1995

We seem to lurch one step forward, only to stagger two back. Jean woke up from her post-lunch doze to see Rachel standing over her, the file of letters in her hand. Apparently, not being able to visit her mother had set her thinking. The question on her mind was whether or not she ought to write.

Naturally, Jean was delighted to be taken into her confidence and determined to make the most of the opportunity. She told me afterwards that her pulse was racing, making it very hard to appear to be talking casually. What the atmosphere must have been like in that room, I dread to think.

Rachel told Jean how she used to write to her father every week when he was in prison. She'd describe life at school, her football prowess, her favourite pop groups and so on. All perfectly normal subjects. Trevor apparently wrote back in the same vein, making jokes and putting in humorous doodles.

Jean decided to do a little gentle pushing and asked if he'd suggested keeping their correspondence a secret, as he hadn't exactly seen eye-to-eye with her mother and sister. Perhaps there was something he didn't want them to see?

Rachel immediately flared up. She accused Jean of going through her things and reading her letters. Unfortunately, I came in at that moment, without any clue of what had just happened. Rachel rounded on me, demanding to know what I'd read.

I was so taken by surprise, I admitted to having taken a glance at one or two. If I live to be a hundred, I'll never forget the hurt, betrayed look in her eyes.

'I trusted you two,' she whispered. 'How could you do it? You had no right.'

Once again, she's completely incommunicado behind a locked bedroom door. There's nothing we can do except wait for her to calm down. I only hope she doesn't destroy the evidence in a fit of rage.

More bad news on the Close, I'm afraid. Following the riot outside the prison gates last week, I hear Rosie Banks was taken ill and has now lost the baby she was carrying. Such a sadness, and all in the name of justice.

13th July 1995

We've blown it completely. Rachel hasn't emerged at all. Trays of breakfast, lunch and dinner have gone cold outside the door. I haven't even seen or heard her go to the toilet. I tried coaxing her out with promises of Monopoly or Scrabble. Sausage and mash, her absolute favourite, brought no response.

What's she doing in there? What's going through her mind? How on earth are we going to get her out?

14th July 1995

I never want to go through another evening like this

one. Jean and I started a campaign of contrition outside Rachel's door. The first glimmer of hope came when I harked back to her babyhood, pointing out how much Mandy loved her then and how she's never stopped.

'It's Beth she loves,' came the muffled response.

I couldn't think what to say. An ominous smell of burning came from under the door. Jean took over. 'This is nonsense,' she said. 'Your mother is serving a life sentence because of you. Because she was prepared to do anything, even to kill, to save you from what happened to Beth. Do you seriously believe she doesn't love you? If there is one thing you can do for your mother and for yourself too, it is to face up to whatever happened between you and your father.'

My heart was pounding so loud I could hardly hear what was going on. I thought, she's really done it now. Why did she have to make it sound like Rachel's to blame? I had a vision of her setting light to each piece of evidence in turn.

We stood there for ages, holding our breaths. In reality, I suppose it was no more than quarter of an hour, but it felt like a lifetime. Then the door opened and Rachel came out, tears streaming down her face. She obviously hadn't slept or changed her clothes. Her hair, normally so sleek and smart, was in rats' tails and mascara was running down her cheeks. She thrust the precious file into my hand.

'I still love my Dad,' she said. 'But when I was very little in the bath, it was just like a game we played. Then when he came out of prison, he was just so alone. I was the only one who . . .' She couldn't finish the sentence. All she could do was swallow a sob and go on. 'I don't have to stop loving him now, do I?'

Without waiting for us to answer, she locked herself in her bedroom again. No amount of coaxing has been able to get her to open the door. The poor girl must be in agonies.

But we've got the letters. The evidence that could free Mandy and Beth Jordache.

17th July 1995

The whole weekend was devoted to looking after Rachel. It was as though she'd retreated almost into babyhood. In the end, we treated her as if she had a nasty bug. Lots of soft food and plenty of good, hot tea. She's been very quiet and tearful, not wanting to talk about it. I can't say I'm surprised. Jean and I decided not to insist on in-depth discussions at this point. She knows we're here if she needs us.

First thing in the morning, Sinbad and I took the letters to Alison Dicks. Frankly, the interview was a terrible disappointment. In her opinion, the letters on their own may indicate that Trevor Jordache's behaviour towards his daughter could have been inappropriate, but Rachel's testimony would be needed to get the full benefit on appeal. If she co-operated, it might be a possible turning point. She emphasized 'might'.

I thought that even without Rachel, the harsh sentence could have been appealed on the provocation issue or self-defence. Unfortunately, it appears we can't simply go back and ask for a second chance. There has to be fresh evidence. It all comes back to Rachel and the letters.

The procedure is incredibly long drawn out. The next stage is for Alison Dicks to contact Mr Anderson, the defence counsel, to get on to the court and ask for a postponement of the appeal on the basis that fresh evidence is being prepared. The prosecution will want proof that Trevor Jordache wrote the letters, so they'll have to be authenticated. I'd have thought the fact that a number of them were written on prison paper would have been sufficient.

Worst of all is the need to involve Rachel. This is only just the beginning, enough to get an appeal granted. Then the fight with the prosecution really begins. The judges have to be convinced that Rachel was raped and that was the core of Mandy and Beth's actions, giving them just cause for killing Trevor. It's all so damned complicated.

Rachel will have to sign a sworn affidavit about what went on between her and her father. The prosecution will maintain that her turnaround is due to guilt and that she's now lying in order to release her mother. It's even possible that they could request a medical examination. I dread to think what her reaction would be to that.

19th July 1995

That poor girl seems to lurch from one crisis to the next. Alison Dicks called round to give me an update. The prosecution have got copies of the letters and are acting in an entirely predictable manner. They've stopped short of asking for a physical examination, but are insisting on a psychiatrist's report.

I can't believe they can be so cruel. Surely the poor girl's been through enough already without having to relive the whole thing in front of a stranger. Even if this quack is highly experienced, it's still going to be a terrible ordeal for her.

There's more. It is almost certain that if the appeal is granted, Rachel will have to go back in the witness box. Her own testimony is crucial, as the prosecution will come up with all manner of theories as to why she's changed her mind. She's got to convince the judges that she's telling the truth now.

I'm only just starting to appreciate how much courage it took for her to face up to what happened. Yet her only reward seems to be ever more heartache.

Rachel was quite appalled when she heard the news. I'm not sure which was worse, the prospect of the psychiatrist or the witness box. The poor girl is under a hell of a lot of pressure. Part of her feels guilty at the thought of betraying her father's memory, yet her co-operation is essential for the appeal. I could see her wavering at the thought of what's still to come. Pray God she can see it through.

20th July 1995

We've been given leave to appeal and the hearing will be held on 25th July 1995. A mere five days away. Now that it's all set, things are really moving. It all hinges on Rachel, though. If she hadn't come forward, the judges said the appeal wouldn't have been granted.

Alison Dicks arranged an appointment for Rachel to see the psychiatrist this morning. I took her to see a Dr Terrence Maclone. He's had over thirty years experience of cases like this, specializing in the effects of child abuse in the home by a member of the immediate family. What an extraordinary way to spend one's working life! Still, he seemed like a good egg.

I was more than a little worried at Rachel having to see him alone. She was in there for nearly two and a half hours. I went right through the three ancient copies of *Country Life* twice over. At one stage, I heard the sounds of crying, even though the waiting room was across the corridor from his office.

When she eventually emerged, Rachel actually looked rather relieved. Her face was more relaxed than it's been for weeks. The receptionist got her a cup of tea, while I took the chance of a brief word with Dr Maclone.

He's convinced that she's telling the truth this time. Apparently, her behaviour demonstrated typical characteristics of someone who's been sexually abused. I asked him why she'd lied in the first place. It was so categorical. I've never been able to understand this tenacious, unswerving loyalty towards a man who behaved so utterly badly towards her.

Dr Maclone said she was probably 'in denial' – an expression which smacked to me of psychological jargon. In layman's terms, she was so deeply upset by what had happened, that she refused to believe it. Rather than confront an overwhelming problem, she pretended it didn't exist. Pushed it to the back of her mind. Shut it out so completely, she genuinely thought she was telling the truth.

This phase can last for years, but in Rachel's case it seems likely that the trauma of the trial and her mother's incarceration brought her out of it. In the end, her love for her mother won out.

22nd July 1995

A chapter of disasters. I agreed to take Sinbad over to Yorkshire to visit Mandy and Beth yesterday. Unfortunately, the Cortina's radiator sprang the tiniest of leaks. I always keep an emergency egg in the boot for just such an eventuality. Old-fashioned it may be, but the science behind it is as revolutionary as ever. The protein in the egg solidifies once it comes into contact with the hot water from the radiator and thus blocks the leak. It's perfect.

We stopped at a service station for me to effect the repair and Sinbad went in search of tea. He came back with some bad news – the motorway was jampacked.

Tailbacks for miles.

Nil desperandum, I thought. I still know some of the alternative roads and we'd have the advantage of an infinitely more picturesque route. I don't wish to cast aspersions on Sinbad's navigational skills, but somehow we missed a vital turning. The man can't even tell the difference between a church with a spire and one with a tower. At one point he even tried to blame it on my trusty map, which I have relied on for years.

I did what should have been a quick three point at the entrance of a field and got stuck fast in the mud. It took a friendly yokel with a tractor to haul us out. We were about to start off when I noticed an ominous wisp of steam coming from the bonnet. I swear it was the wretched farm vehicle that did the damage. That radiator had been absolutely A1 when we left the service station. Suffice it to say, we had to call out the emergency breakdown service and be towed ignominiously to the nearest garage. It then transpired we couldn't be taken back to Liverpool, as the chap had to go to some sheepdog trials.

There was only one thing to do. Book into the local B&B and wait till morning. It's not an experience I wish to repeat. I do not appreciate sharing a bed with a man who snores.

25th July 1995

I hardly know what I'm writing. I feel in a state of complete shock. Bewildered. Confused. Angry. Numb.

How did it happen? One minute we were on our way to London, buoyed up by the thought of Mandy and Beth gaining their freedom. The next, we're in mourning.

I can't tell the story. The pen keeps sliding out of my hands. The paper looks unreal. I don't know what I'm doing.

I've got to carry on. I've got to get what happened sorted out in my mind. Make sense of this appalling thing.

Rachel and I came down to London last night to prepare for the appeal. It was due to start at 10am today. We got there in plenty of time. We had to pass through a barrage of journalists, photographers and TV cameras. A large crowd had gathered, a mixture of well-wishers and protesters. The case has been appropriated by all sorts of groups with an axe to grind. A cheer went up as Rachel appeared.

We were shown into an elegant, oak-panelled waiting room. We waited and waited. Ten o'clock came and went. Eleven o'clock. Noon. There was no sign of Sinbad or anyone else for the defence. Periodically, I went in search of an usher, but they were as ignorant as we were. All they could say was that there'd been a delay. Rachel pretended to read her book, I held the *Telegraph* in front of my face. Neither of us could cope with idle chit-chat.

At 1pm, Sinbad appeared. One glance at his face was enough to see that disaster had struck. The plain, bald truth is that Beth Jordache died suddenly in the night. She'd been taken ill, rushed to the hospital wing and simply passed away. At the moment, no-one knows what possible cause there could be. How could a healthy, vigorous nineteen year old just stop breathing like that?

Sinbad took Rachel off to see Mandy. Then came more hours of waiting. I telephoned Jean to report back. It was a horrible call. I couldn't think of anything to say. Silence is appalling over the phone wires. Jean was all for rushing down to London, but I told her we'd probably be back tonight, so there was no point. I wish I'd let her come now. I feel so alone.

We're still in London. The appeal is going ahead on Friday. The judges agreed a couple of days adjournment, but if proceedings don't start then, a new date will have to be fixed. That could take months – we were extremely lucky with this one. As brutal as it sounds, a tragedy like this might be a lifesaver. The sympathy vote might not count for much six months down the line.

Sinbad was distraught when he told me. Mandy's in a terrible state, of course. She's not fit to sit in court, hearing evidence about one daughter being abused while the other lies on a slab in the morgue. However, she's even less fit to stay a minute longer than she has to behind bars. Either the appeal starts now or Mandy grieves alone in her prison cell.

Rachel spent the afternoon with Mandy and Sinbad. There was nothing for me to do, but potter round the shops. I can't remember a single item in a single window. I retired to the hotel, where Rachel joined me for dinner. Not that we ate anything. We spent the rest of the evening together in silence. Rachel just sat gazing out of the window, tears pouring down her face. I couldn't open my mouth for fear I'd start howling myself.

28th July 1995

It's finally over. The appeal was successful and Mandy is free. Everything went like clockwork. It was obvious that everyone, including the judges and the prosecution, was sympathetic towards the grieving widow.

In his opening speech, Mr Tate acting for the prosecution went through all the arguments Miss Dicks warned us about. The letters were trivial, Rachel is now lying etc. etc. He called the new evidence at best flimsy and at worst inconsequential. Yet he sounded distinctly half-hearted, quite unlike the sharp, angry tones that rang out over Liverpool Crown Court.

The whole thing was completed in a morning. First came two undisputed reports from graphologists, stating that the letters were indeed written by Trevor Jordache. Then Dr Maclone took the stand and repeated his conviction that Rachel was telling the truth when she said her father had abused her. Again, the prosecution barely commented.

The last person to be called was Rachel. Mr Anderson QC took her through the evidence as gently as he could.

My heart went out to her as she told how her father's abuse escalated after he wormed his way into number 10, Brookside Close. The man was utterly evil. He used his own daughter's love for him to hurt her in the most vile way.

Rachel described how he said she was his favourite, all he had. He needed comfort, someone to make him feel better, someone to keep him warm and hold him. The blame was laid at Mandy's door, because she wouldn't let him near her. Once he'd established himself in Rachel's bed, he gradually became more and more revoltingly intimate. And more and more powerful. Rachel became too scared to cry or tell anyone what was happening. Her father warned her that it was all her fault and no-one would believe her. Then he raped her.

You could have heard a pin drop as she told her tale. When the prosecution got up to cross-examine, he only had two questions.

'Are you fully aware of the importance of the evidence you have given this court?' was the first.

Rachel said she was.

'You have nothing more to say about the relationship between you and your father?'

'He raped me.'

Mr Tate had no further questions.

The judges took less than an hour to reach their decision. When Mandy emerged a free woman, the crowd cheered, but she hardly seemed to notice them. Sinbad and Alison Dicks hustled her back to the hotel. She made a press statement from there.

'Today I was freed by the court of appeal. They finally decided that I was right in defending myself and my daughters by killing my husband. I'd like to thank all my friends and all those people who campaigned for my release and everyone who's supported me over the past few months. But the one person that I'd really like to thank should be standing here beside me today, my daughter, Beth. It's because of her strength and courage that I am a free woman today. From day one, it was Beth who protested our innocence. It was she who inspired the campaign to free us. She never gave up hope. She never stopped believing in her own innocence. And it was her determination that kept us going through our darkest hours. This should have been her moment of victory. I don't want anyone to forget the name Beth Jordache and I intend to start an appeal in her name for women's refuges. In this way, none of us will forget what Beth Jordache did for women in this country.'

I didn't always see eye to eye with Beth, but she was a courageous and determined girl. She deserved a far better fate. How could such an apparently healthy young girl die so suddenly like that? I didn't dare verbalise it, but it did cross my mind that in desperation and fearing an unsuccessful appeal, she took her own life.

5th August 1995

Things are gradually calming down. I was going to say 'getting back to normal', but I don't know what's normal these days. The coroner has issued the release for burial order for Beth. Sinbad's arranged the funeral for next Tuesday.

It seems that Beth's death was a bizarre legacy from Trevor. She died of hypertrophic cardio-myopathy, where the muscles of the heart thicken up and prevent it from functioning normally. It's a genetic condition. According to the medical records, there's a history of it in the Jordache family. There will have to be an inquest, of course, but that will be just a formality in a few months time. Death by natural causes.

The tragedy has brought Mandy and Rachel together again. Although she's decided to stay with us, Rachel spends most of her waking hours with her mother and Sinbad. It's good to see the three of them together, even with the pall of grief hanging over them.

The ritual of the funeral arrangements has helped. Rachel went with Mandy to the chapel of rest to say her goodbyes to Beth. She came back very calm and peaceful. It's as if she's crossed the threshold into adulthood. She's offered to do one of the readings at the service. I'm sure she'll make an excellent job of it. Mandy has asked me to be one of the pallbearers. I told her I'd be honoured.

There's still another ordeal for the poor girl to go through. Because Beth's condition was hereditary, it's vital for Rachel to get checked out. Mandy's made an appointment for her to see the specialist at the hospital and will go with her. Jean and I felt quite a pang when she told us the plan. Of course, it's wonderful that Rachel and Mandy are reconciled, but we'll miss having her exclusively as our daughter.

8th August 1995

Beth has been laid to rest. The funeral went very well. The church was full of family and friends. Luckily, the press and sightseers kept away. Alison Dicks was there. She's become quite a friend of Mandy's. Lots of Beth's fellow students from the university came, although she'd been away for such a long time. I wondered which, among her female friends, were of the same sexual persuasion. Patricia joined myself and Jean. Max said he was too busy, which caused a bit of friction between him and Patsy.

The coffin was carried in by myself and Sinbad at the front, with Mick Johnson and Mike Dixon at the back. As I put my shoulder under the wood, I prayed for forgiveness for the uncharitable and harsh clashes I'd had with Beth since she announced she was a lesbian. Somehow, all that stuff didn't seem to matter any more.

Rachel's reading was taken from the *Gospel According To St. Mark*, chapter 10. 'Suffer the little children to come unto me and forbid them not. For of such is the kingdom of God.' After saying those words, Rachel couldn't continue. It was as if the realization of her sister's death really hit home at that moment. Beth, the sharer of her childhood, had gone never to return. They will never meet again in this life.

Mike Dixon made a heroic effort and took over. He finished the reading, then gave us an ex tempore speech of his own. 'I suppose those are the official words, but from where I'm standing, I find it hard to believe it's the last time I'll be in the same room as me mate, Beth. I think the really good thing about today is all the people here who were really close to her. Not the telly cameras. Not the journalists. Not anything. Just people who knew her. People who loved her. I know, because of what she went through that she was picked up and used by loads of good causes. Some people see her as the girl who stood up with her mum and fought back. Other people see her for her sexuality, as a lesbian. Everyone who's read the papers may think they knew her, but they don't. At the end of the day, she was just Beth to us. A symbol of light and hope. The girl I fell in love with. What I'm trying to say is that Beth was first and foremost a person. She's not here to look after her mum and her kid sister. I'm sure everyone here will try and help you through all this. Because these are your real friends.'

He stood there, in the face of that congregation, letting his tears flow freely. I'd always thought of him as Ron Dixon's son, but I realized then that he too has grown up. Whatever his political persuasion, he's become a fine young man. Beth would have been proud to have heard him. I confess I had to make use of my handkerchief. Jean openly sobbed in my arms.

At the grave, each person present threw in a single red carnation. It was a touching gesture. Mandy was the last. She held on to that flower as if she couldn't bear to let it go. My heart went out to her. For a second, I could imagine the utter, bewildering loss of a child dying. I looked at Patricia, alive and grieving, and I was almost overcome by love and fear for her.

10 *August* 1995

Rachel had to go to the hospital for the tests today. She returned very thoughtful and quiet. The only information we could elicit was that they'd done a load of tests, as she described it, and that the results will be available in a week. I thought the turnaround was pretty good, but Rachel was dismayed at the wait.

Surely nothing more can go wrong for her. Hasn't she suffered enough? She's starting to get her appetite back and to sleep a little better. The last thing she needs is to be in fear of her own life.

There has been another disturbing development on the Close. Brenna Jordache has turned up again. How that woman has the nerve to show her face, I don't know. Sinbad came to see me positively fuming. He and Mandy had bumped into her outside the house. All she wanted to do was talk – or so she said. Personally, I wouldn't trust that woman further than I could throw a grand piano.

Mandy sent her away with a flea in her ear, but she was back the next day, hammering and banging on the front door fit to wake the dead. I confess my attention was caught by the noise and I got a peek at her from behind the blinds. Mandy opened the door, but after a very few moments' discussion, slammed it again. Brenna waited outside for a while, then retreated. I spotted her skulking behind some bushes a good couple of hours later. What on earth can the woman be up to this time?

11th August 1995

Could I have misjudged Brenna Jordache? Mandy gave in to her pleadings and gave her a brief audience. Her tale did make a certain amount of sense, especially when remembering what the psychiatrist said about Rachel being 'in denial'.

It seems that Jordache senior, Rachel's grandfather, was a brute of the first order. He terrorized Brenna and Trevor, making their childhood an absolute misery. They had to endure daily beatings for the smallest misdemeanours. To prove the veracity of her story, Brenna pulled up her clothing to reveal a mass of hideous scars across her back. Even Sinbad was shocked. Mandy was completely convinced.

It doesn't excuse what either Brenna or Trevor did, but it does go some way to explaining it. However, Brenna denied her father ever sexually abused her. That particular perversion was Trevor's alone.

I think Sinbad told me about it to let off steam. Even if Brenna's telling the truth, he doesn't want her around. She's caused too much trouble. I must say, I'm inclined to agree with him.

Rachel takes a completely different attitude. She was always fond of her auntie and it must have been a great shock to discover how malignant she'd been. For her sake, I hope Brenna's intentions are honourable this time.

16th August 1995

Brenna has been round several more times. I do believe she and Mandy have patched things up between them. I suppose it's a good thing. At any rate, Rachel's pleased. Quite apart from anything else, Brenna has been taking a number of the household chores off Mandy's hands. With the baby's arrival imminent, this must be something of a relief. Rachel reports that the atmosphere over the road is warming up considerably. She certainly appreciates her aunt's cooking.

Sinbad is still wary, though. Yesterday, Brenna paid another visit, only to find the house empty. Patricia kindly let her wait in her living room, where she could keep an eye out for the return of the inhabitants. On reflection, however, she wondered if she'd done the right thing and asked Sinbad about it.

He made it clear he'd rather she'd not been quite so friendly to Brenna. No invitation had ever been extended, despite the fact that Brenna is there every other day on average. What really irks him is the way she acts as though nothing untoward has ever happened. He puts Mandy's willingness to forgive down to her regard for Rachel's wellbeing. She was painfully caught between the two sides of the family over the trial and Mandy doesn't want that situation to continue. Patricia suggested that the recent tragic events might have made her realize her brother wasn't such a saint. Maybe she truly regrets being so against Mandy. But Sinbad was adamant. As far as he's concerned, Brenna is incapable of change.

19th August 1995

It's just as well Brenna has taken root chez Mandy and Sinbad. Mandy is decidedly under the weather. Gone down with a nasty tummy bug. Nothing serious, but one can't be too careful during pregnancy. Poor Rachel was very concerned about her mother, but I'm sure there's nothing to worry about. I assured her that this didn't appear to be a return of the mystery virus. Sinbad called in the GP, but apart from reassurance, there was little he could do. In her condition, Mandy would be unwise to take any drugs. The main thing is for someone to be there to keep an eye on her and make sure she gets plenty of fluid. Sinbad's working and Rachel's at school, so Brenna is the ideal person. In being so helpful now, perhaps she's trying to earn her forgiveness. A completely laudable motive.

Attention has been focusing on next door at number 5. It's been empty since Barry Grant high-tailed it for Florida. Jimmy Corkhill has been popping in every now and then, as Barry's gopher and Beverley gives the place a thorough going over with a mop once a week, but otherwise there's been no sign of life. This morning, a workman appeared to do some work on the door. It's all highly mysterious. Perhaps Barry is returning at last.

Max and Patricia will be relieved to see him. Although Max would like nothing better than to run the restaurant single-handed, having his official business partner AWOL for such a long period causes problems. Also, it would be a good idea to sort out a proper lease on the Gift Box. The shop's doing pretty well now, definitely making a profit, but without Barry's express permission for it to be there, legally speaking Patsy is squatting.

21st August 1995

A letter arrived for Rachel from the hospital. She dashed round to her mother's to open it, leaving us worried sick. Jean and I spent a very uncomfortable half an hour waiting for her to come back. We simply sat staring at our coffees. However, Rachel then came running in, shouting, 'It's OK. I'm clear.' She hugged us both, then ran straight out again.

It's such a relief the whole episode's over. When we'd

recovered from the shock, Jean and I positively wept for joy. The past is surely behind us at last. With Mandy free, Rachel healthy and the family together again, perhaps we can all start to look to the future with optimism.

Rachel graced us with her presence again at supper, beaming all over her face. She had more good news to impart. Mandy has agreed to marry Sinbad and the wedding's set for Friday, 1st September 1995. This is an excellent move. I'm glad Sinbad is so keen to make an honest woman of her. Not to mention the advantages to the baby of being born legitimate. People nowadays think far too little of such things. It's no wonder the moral fabric of our society is collapsing.

It doesn't leave a lot of time for preparation, even though Mandy insists on a quiet do. Jean and I have been racking our brains trying to think of a suitable present. Brenna has practically taken over, from what I can gather. She's down on her luck herself at the moment. It seems she was made redundant from her job a couple of weeks ago and now she's been made homeless as well. Obviously, without work she can't afford to pay the rent. Rachel said she's been dropping large hints about wanting to stay with Mandy and Sinbad for a while until she gets herself sorted out. She's a trained midwife, so it shouldn't be too hard for her to get another job. Rachel's all for the idea, but Mandy and Sinbad find it difficult enough to cope with her being there during waking hours, let alone at night.

Max and Patricia have received something of a blow. It seems that Barry Grant will not be coming back. He's handed over his business affairs in England to an old chum of his from Birmingham to sort out. Apparently, he wants to sell the lot. This friend of his, one Dil Parmar, is causing all sorts of problems. He's an Asian chappie, very young, very smart and very wealthy.

With regard to Grants Restaurant, Barry has offered Max first refusal in buying him out. I must say it sounds like a superb opportunity. He and Patricia have made an appointment with their bank manager and are prepared to take a risk. I went round to see them this evening, to find them poring over the computer, accounts sheets spread all over the floor. They've only got twenty-one days to put in a bid. Let's hope they can do it in time.

23rd August 1995

The peace of our quiet evening in front of the telly was shattered by a very disturbing incident. I had just settled down in front of *Crimewatch*, when there was a terrific hammering on the front door. In an emergency, people seem incapable of using a bell.

I opened up to find Ron Dixon on the doorstep, supporting Brenna Jordache, who was in a terrible state. He'd found her staggering up the pathway between the Parade and the Close. A bunch of yobbos had attacked her and snatched her bag. The poor woman's face was badly grazed and she was very shaken.

Rachel fetched the first-aid kit, while I put the kettle on for some hot, sweet tea. I don't know what this area's coming to. Despite the activities of the Neighbourhood Watch and the B.R.A., situations like this crop up more and more frequently. It's not just our neighbourhood, either. The whole country's going to rack and ruin. Of course, it's all down to television putting ideas into young people's heads. In my young day, no-one would have dreamt of attacking a defenceless woman.

After an hour or so, Miss Jordache had recovered sufficiently to make a few plans. She's had to leave her flat and had booked into a local B&B. Naturally, it was out of the question for her to go anywhere by herself after being mugged. Unfortunately, with Rachel in the spare room, it was impossible for Jean and myself to offer her hospitality. I must say I was glad to have the excuse. I don't feel comfortable in that woman's presence.

Rachel insisted on taking her aunt over to Sinbad's. He was fast asleep by the time she got there, but Mandy was still up. At first, she adamantly refused to allow Brenna to sleep under her roof. It took a lot of persuading before Rachel could get her to relent. What finally swung it was the fact that Brenna had lost all her money. Not only could she not pay for her lodging, she hadn't a penny to pay a cab to get her there.

25th August 1995

Sinbad has reluctantly agreed to let Brenna Jordache stay for a few days. He insists she must be out of the way by the wedding, however. I can't say I blame him.

Personally, I think he's gone above and beyond the call of duty.

That house is getting ridiculously full. While Mandy was offering succour to Brenna, Sinbad had taken on Mick Johnson's two children. They're a lively pair, I must say. This act of altruism stemmed from a desire of Sinbad's to aid and abet Mick's love life. He has an assignation arranged for tonight. I wonder if it's with the school teacher Mick so hotly denied being attached to.

To add insult to injury, the appalling Mr Corkhill has foisted his presence on the household. It seems Jackie has come to her senses and sent him packing. Dil Parmar allowed him to spend a night in the office of La Luz, but told him in no uncertain terms to make his own arrangements after that. I must say I was surprised he was so easily manipulated. He didn't strike me as a soft touch. Sinbad made it clear that Corkhill must be on his way tomorrow, but I fear once the tick has found a willing piece of flesh, he'll cling on with all his might.

30th August 1995

I thought so. I've just reread my last entry. What I predicted has come to pass. Jimmy Corkhill is still firmly ensconced. There is a certain amount of justice in the world, however. He appears to have caught Mandy's bug and has been letting everyone in on the precise state of his bowels. The man is a complete outsider.

Rachel is at a very low ebb. Her GCSE results arrived.

Frankly, they were abysmal. All Es. It's hardly surprising, considering the conditions under which she took the wretched exams. Unfortunately, Rachel doesn't see it like that. Her attitude is that she's 'crap' and didn't want to do them in the first place anyway. Mandy has been doing her best to bolster her confidence, but to no avail. This has put the kibosh on Rachel's returning to school completely. She won't countenance the idea of resitting. I suppose the next step is to haunt the job centre, along with many others of today's youth.

Mandy herself is far from well. Whatever this infection is, it's proving damned hard to get rid of. Rachel is spending a lot of time over there and reporting that her mother was absolutely shattered. I'm surprised at Sinbad allowing Jimmy Corkhill house room when Mandy needs all the peace and quiet she can get. Apparently Brenna is insisting on doing all the cooking herself.

Despite the problems, the wedding plans are going ahead. Sinbad has asked Mick Johnson to be his best man. I'm sure he'll do an excellent job. I shan't easily forget his stoic reliability during the epidemic crisis. Definitely a man you can rely on.

Brenna has taken charge of the wedding cake. Rachel spent a most enjoyable afternoon helping her with the icing. Took her mind off things. I must say it looks magnificent. The design is simple, but excellently executed. Mike Dixon has also come up trumps, volunteering to video the ceremony as a present. He's hoping to turn professional, so this will be good practice for him.

31st August 1995

Max and Patricia treated us to an excellent lunch at Grants. Splendid Rioja and as for the Cognac . . . ! The restaurant was gratifyingly full. Since Max introduced special lunchtime menus, they've been getting jolly busy.

There was, however, an ulterior motive. The meeting with the bank manager last week was only a partial success. They've been offered a loan, but it isn't enough. Could Jean and I help out? Max warned that they need a lot of money, possibly all of our life's savings.

The trouble is, Jean and I ploughed the vast majority of our capital into the bungalow. When we counted it up, we found that our total realizable assets consist of Jean's £2,000 in the Post Office, my £1,500 in granny bonds and gas shares worth about £500. It was obviously nowhere near enough. Max and Patricia didn't tell us the exact shortfall, but their faces dropped.

Mr Dil Parmar appeared to look around. Max became terribly flustered at his entrance. They were having a bit of a barney under their breaths, when who should show up, but Jimmy Corkhill. With Cracker! On top of all of his other shortcomings, the man doesn't even have the most basic sense of hygiene. Max ended up raising his voice and telling both of them they're barred. It seems Mr Parmar wants to put in a bid for Barry's half of the restaurant and was putting pressure on Max.

I feel so sorry for Patsy and Max. Grants is a gilt-edged investment. They've got so many plans for it. It would be a dream come true – running a family business, making all the decisions with no outside interference. If only we could help out.

1st September 1995

Will nothing ever go right for the Jordache family? Today was supposed to be the big one. Sinbad and Mandy getting married. The bungalow was a hive of activity from first light. I couldn't get into the bathroom until well after nine with Rachel and Jean hogging it.

Rachel had a little weep at one stage. She said it seemed 'weird' not having Beth around. In the old days, they'd always prepared for special occasions together. Rachel would purloin Beth's make-up. Beth would shout, but let her little sister have her own way in the end.

I'm sure it did the poor girl a world of good to reminisce a bit. She's determined to put the past behind her and get on with her life, but even she realizes grief doesn't simply vanish overnight. I think she was worried about the changes her mother's marriage might make. Jean broached the subject of Rachel moving back with Mandy and Sinbad, but she doesn't want to. Even though she and Mandy have got over their differences, she wants a degree of separation. Frankly, I'm delighted. She can stay here as long as she likes.

Mandy was supposed to come with us, but Brenna said she wasn't quite ready and that they'd follow on in a taxi. We met Sinbad at the registry office, absolutely pale with last-minute nerves. Mick Johnson hadn't turned up either, so the poor chap was standing all alone on the steps, feeling totally abandoned.

The minutes ticked by and neither Mandy nor Mick appeared. It was most embarrassing. Another two couples went in, their parties staring at ours, wondering what was going on. Sinbad was in a terrible state. He borrowed Max's mobile phone, but couldn't get through to either of the missing persons. Had Mandy's illness taken a turn for the worse? Could she have gone into labour? Why hadn't she sent Brenna with a message?

Eventually, the registrar had to call the whole thing off. She was most apologetic, but her timetable didn't allow her to wait any longer. We drove back to the Close in record time. Jean and I thought it best to drift off and leave Sinbad and Rachel to it.

They had to break into the house, as Sinbad had forgotten his keys. Rachel discovered Mandy lying unconscious at the foot of the stairs, with an angry red mark on her temple. There was no sign of Brenna. An ambulance was summoned and Mandy was whisked into hospital. We'll know more about what happened tomorrow.

2nd September 1995

It's unbelievable! That witch Brenna had actually been trying to poison Mandy and the unborn child. She deliberately wormed her way into the house, so she could wreak her twisted revenge for her brother's death. And this is the woman who had the nerve to talk about the comfort of her Catholicism. She ought to be excommunicated instantly. All the while she was pretending to minister to Mandy's needs, she was adding doses of some noxious substance to her tea and meals.

Thank God Mandy and the baby are alright. Sinbad blames himself for having been taken in, but we all were. He's furious with Brenna and not too pleased with Mandy. She refuses to inform the police, even though the woman's obviously a menace to society. In a way, I can understand it. She's been through so much over the past months, she can't face the thought of another police station or court room. For once, Sinbad's going to have to let her do things her way. They've decided to take the honeymoon anyway and put the ceremony off for a while. A holiday in the Lake District will do them both good.

There's no sign of Mick Johnson. He appears to have done a runner. I must say I'm surprised at him. He always seemed like such a reliable, dependable sort. Not the type to run off without a word to anyone. Ron Dixon's not best pleased – he's been left with Mick's two children, having agreed to babysit for the wedding. I dare say Mick's had an emergency, although it's odd he hasn't even phoned in.

6th September 1995

Still no sign of Mick. It's been four days now and Ron's going frantic. Strictly speaking, the Parade is outside the B.R.A.'s jurisdiction, but I popped up as a neighbour to see if there was any sign of life. I knocked and listened. Nothing. Ron's been going up there regularly, too.

The latest rumour is that he's chasing after some floozie. I suspect that school teacher, Jenny Swift. It's thoroughly irresponsible of him. You don't simply dump your children with a neighbour and waltz off. Not if you don't want to get into hot water with the social services.

Besides, Patricia pays to use his van for Gift Box deliveries. I was stuck without proper transport this morning, as Mick hadn't even the courtesy to leave me the keys. I had to make four round trips in the Cortina. The upholstery will never be the same again.

I came across PC Coburn off duty in the Parade. I asked him if he'd investigate as our community police officer. He was reassuring and promised to look in on Mick on his way home. Now it's in the hands of the police, I feel I've done my bit.

Max is tearing his hair out about Grants. He was positively pleading with me to help him find the money to buy out Barry. Jimmy Corkhill, of all people, has indicated he wishes to put in a bid. It may be some perverted way of getting at him, of course, but perhaps he really has got a pot of gold stashed away. One thing's for sure. If he has, it wasn't come by honestly.

I don't think that Indian chappie would be all that

bad. Damn sight better than the awful Corkhill. They're very hard workers. A proud people. Max still looked dubious. I fear he can be a tad prejudiced. He does have rather a bad habit of patronizing the natives.

The poor man was so desperate, he was even talking of selling his share. It would be a tragedy after all the hard work he and Patricia have put into it.

8th September 1995

Corkhill's moved on to the Close. After everything he's done, he's had the brass neck to buy number 10 from Sinbad. I'm completely appalled at the thought of having him as a neighbour. Property prices will plummet.

If he's got that kind of money, he could well be serious about buying Barry's share of Grants. Patricia's heartbroken. Max could make a go of it if he had the place to himself. If he has to share with some stranger, his heart won't be in it. And if the new partner turned out to be Jimmy Corkhill . . . The idea's unthinkable.

They made an eleventh-hour plea to the bank without success. They know the restaurant has enough collateral to secure the loan, but they're cowardly when it comes to small businesses. The shortfall is some £30,000. I had no idea it was so much.

I've got to do something to help. There's only one thing for it. The bungalow is bought and paid for. Jean and I can raise the money the children need by remortgaging it. Max and Patricia would take care of the repayments, using the profits from the restaurant.

I put the proposal to Jean and she flatly refused to consider it. You'd have thought her recent brush with death would have made her more altruistic, but it's had quite the opposite effect. She said she'd reached an age where she can be a bit more selfish. Then she started harping on about wanting to travel and see something of the world. I don't know how she can be so hard-hearted.

Mick is still AWOL and now PC Coburn's disappeared. It's very mysterious. He always phones or calls round if I report anything to him. Still, now that the police are involved, it's out of my hands. I've got other things to think about. Poor Ron is not happy at all. As well as being saddled with Mick's offspring, he now has Jimmy Corkhill as a neighbour. If he's not careful he'll have a heart attack.

10th September 1995

Once again Brookside Close has been the focus of media attention. It turns out that Mick Johnson was being held captive. We were right about one thing – it was Miss Swift. The poor girl developed a fixation on our Pizza king to such an extent she ended up pulling a gun on him in a jealous rage. I've heard of such things happening before. Apparently, it's an extremely rare condition and she'll probably end up in a mental institution.

When PC Coburn failed to report back, Ron and I

decided to try the flat one last time. We knocked and this time heard the sound of voices coming from inside. One was definitely female and she was obviously very upset. There was the noise of a scuffle and then a shot rang out.

Ron and I ran for help. In minutes the Parade was under siege. The shops were evacuated. The salon's clients weren't even given a chance to rinse the shampoo out. We were all herded behind a blue-and-white taped line. Crack police marksmen were stationed around the flat. Other officers with riot shields were standing by.

As chairman of the B.R.A., I immediately offered my services to the man in charge, one Chief Inspector Wallis. I then detailed Jean to fetch supplies of good hot coffee, as it looked like we were in for a long wait. She objected to the menial task, until I pointed out that as the residents' elected representative, it was my duty to stand by in case the police needed my help.

Chief Inspector Wallis tried to contact the flat using a megaphone. No reply. They put an open phone line by the entrance, but everything went quiet.

Hours later, there was another shot. The police converged on the Pizza Parlour from all sides. The next thing we knew, an ambulance drew up and a stretcher taken out of it. Then, a figure emerged flanked by officers and covered in a blanket. Mick followed. They were bundled into a police car and that was that.

We heard over the radio that a woman was being held and that a policeman had been wounded by gunshot, but those of us on the ground, so to speak, were kept completely in the dark. I must say, I feel this was a trifle unfair, given our total co-operation.

It's funny how so much excitement can be so tedious. Absolutely nothing happened. I found my thoughts wandering, particularly in the direction of Grants restaurant. With only a few hours to go before the deadline, I made a decision. If Jean was not prepared to help, then I'd have to go it alone. I informed Patricia and Max that we were willing to mortgage the bungalow. They were delighted and faxed Barry straight away. It'll take me a few days to sort out the details, but it does mean they can put in the offer. Jean need never know, as the Farnhams will be taking care of the repayments.

15th September 1995

I'm in the doghouse once again. I hadn't bargained for Patricia's demonstrative gratitude. She came round to the bungalow proffering chocolates and champagne before I had a chance to stop her and explain.

Jean launched into a tirade as soon as Patsy left. She called me utterly despicable and selfish. Selfish! Me! They were desperate. Max could have ended up with that clown, Corkhill, as his partner. We were their only option.

I decided a strategic withdrawal was in order, so I went to visit PC Coburn in hospital. He was sitting up and taking notice. Apparently, the school marm shot him in the arm as he was trying to calm her down. The doctor says he should be up and about in a few weeks.

I have to take some of the blame on my shoulders for what happened. If I'd had any idea it was such a dangerous situation, I'd never have sent him to investigate.

In my opinion, his bravery deserves an OBE. I fully expected him to tell me his superiors had been in touch to reward him with early promotion. On the contrary. He's actually been reprimanded for going off duty without letting his station know. It's outrageous! No wonder law and order in this country are in such a dreadful state.

19th September 1995

Mick's back home, but he hasn't opened up the Pizza Parlour yet. The siege has had a dramatic effect on him. He's a changed man, sullen, defensive and tense. His children, Leo and Gemma, haven't been seen. Several neighbours have reported their offers of help being rebuffed. He probably just needs time to get over the trauma.

I went with him to the magistrate's court today, as there was a bail hearing for Jenny Swift. Naturally, it wasn't granted. The magistrates made some pertinent comments about the use of guns in our society. It is truly appalling the way people can pick up firearms just like that.

20th September 1995

That bloody Corkhill goes from bad to worse. This morning, I caught him attaching a massive radio aerial to his roof. I went straight over to find out what's going on. He's only planning to run a taxi business from his newly acquired property!

The whole thing's impossible. He'd already got several vehicles in various states of disrepair parked in the Close. I'm damn sure it's against council regulations and I'll eat my hat if he's got a licence.

As chairman of the B.R.A., it is clearly my duty to do something about this. We can't have our peaceful neighbourhood turned into a taxi stand with cars coming and going at all hours of the day and night. What about the children? Brookside Close is not a through road. The extra traffic would be downright dangerous.

I went straight down to the library to check out the regulations. I was right. Corkhill needs a licence and planning permission. It's completely contrary to the leasing arrangements on the house for him to operate that sort of a business from it. I shall be having a word with that miscreant as soon as possible.

While I was in town, I had a brainwave. Jean is still barely talking to me. When she does deign to speak, it's to complain again about her humdrum, stay-at-home life. She's picked up some book about a woman travelling through the more inaccessible parts of the Himalayas. Sounds very uncomfortable and extremely cold, but Jean always has had a romantic streak. There is no way we are crossing the Hindu Kush on a mule nor are we going down the Amazon in a hollowed-out tree trunk.

However, we do need a holiday and I feel I ought to make it up to Jean for pulling the wool over her eyes re the loan to Max and Patsy. I found the very thing in the travel agent's. A weekend in Bath with Golden Oldies, specialists in services for the over-sixties. They put you up in the finest hotel, wine and dine you every night and provide a coach and guide for some of the finest neo-classical architecture in Europe. It's an excellent deal, so I booked up straight away. We leave in three weeks time. Jean looked a little disappointed when I told her, but she'll come round.

22nd September 1995

Jean and Rosie have come up with an excellent scheme. The Banks and the Crosbies have formed a syndicate to play the Lottery. If only we could hit the jackpot, Jean would forgive me for taking out the mortgage on the bungalow. The four of us pool our resources, thus giving ourselves four times the chances of winning.

I decided a little research was in order. There are a number of informative tomes on the market, giving details of various systems. I must say Eddie took quite a lot of convincing. He and Rosie had simply picked numbers based on the family's birthdays.

However, if you study the winning numbers drawn so

far, the chances of winning using dates, i.e. numbers below thirty-two, are considerably less than by using all the numbers available. I discovered an ally in young Lee. Armed with my new companion at the keyboard, we soon came up with a suitable formula. We've cut the odds down from 13,983,816:1 to 3,500,000:1. I'm certain we're on to a winner. Tomorrow's the big day.

23rd September 1995

I knew it. A tenner first go. Of course, that's only £2.50 each, but it's the principle that counts. Next week could be the big one. Ron showed himself a trifle envious when I told him, but he has troubles of his own. His daughter, Jacqui, has taken over the hair salon and is expanding into the flat above the Trading Post. She's going to be opening a beauty parlour. As a father, Ron's pleased as punch, but as a trader, he's worried about the disruption to his business. He had a touch of angina a few weeks ago and really ought to be taking care of his blood pressure. Unfortunately, he seems to be on a very short fuse.

Corkhill's at the bottom of it. The sheer effrontery of the man knows no bounds. He can hardly expect to be invited to tea by the neighbours. Only a year ago, he was entering their properties uninvited and departing with the VCR under his arm. As for the tragic affair of young Tony Dixon, Ron will never be able to forgive him for that. I'm sure I couldn't in his place. Corkhill's drug-crazed driving was responsible for Tony's fatal accident. No amount of remorse, simulated or otherwise, can wipe the slate clean. If he was truly sorry for what he did, he'd keep out of the way.

I've been trying to question him about this wretched minicab affair, but he's proving most elusive. Patches of oil have sprung up all over the Close. Something will have to be done.

26th September 1995

Success. In a week's time, the Close will once again be a haven of peace and tranquillity. At least, as far as taxis are concerned. I finally ran Corkhill to ground and demanded to see his operating licence and planning permission. Naturally, he couldn't provide either one, despite a lot of bluster. He even had the cheek to call into question the validity of the B.R.A. I should think a case like this only goes to prove it's the lifeblood of the community.

I allowed him seven days' grace to find new premises. If he's still operating then, I shall be forced into taking the necessary steps. I will not hesitate to ask the appropriate authorities to seek a legal order banning him from trading. That should do it. I'm sure everyone will be vastly relieved at the good news.

27th September 1995

More trouble with vehicles. A thoroughly disreputable caravan has been parked on the Parade. No registration number, of course, and the thing is falling to bits. Ron helped me investigate and the door-handle came away in his hand. There wasn't any sign of life. I hope it doesn't presage the influx of a load of undesirable people.

I didn't have time to do anything more about it. Max and Patricia held a relaunch of Grants. A celebration of their sole ownership. It was absolutely first class. A glut of gastronomic gratification. I was quite amazed what could be done with a hunk of humble tuna fish.

The tenor of the restaurant has changed from British through and through to something called Cal Ital. Max explained it to me. The idea is to take the best of Italian tastes and ingredients and mix it with Californian-style cooking and presentation. I couldn't quite work out which bit was meant to be Cal and which Ital, but it all went down very well. We had a choice of wine from both regions and I made sure I had a thorough sampling of each. Jean drove home.

30th September 1995

Talk about from the sublime to the ridiculous. The secret of the mysterious caravan was revealed. It's Corkhill's latest attempt at running a business. He's planning to run his taxi service from that monstrosity! I might have known. That out and out villain is incapable of doing anything legitimate.

He held his own version of a launching ceremony. Two bottles of Asti Spumante, a lot of raucous ribaldry and a quick snap by the local free-sheet hack. Naturally, I remonstrated with him. All he's done is to move his blasted eyesore from the Close to the Parade. It's outrageous. He must surely be contravening some byelaw or other. His visual pollution will not go unchallenged.

Ron was absolutely furious. I swear I could see the steam pouring from his ears. In fact, his vehemence was so strong, I had to warn him against taking matters into his own hands. I don't want the good name of the B.R.A. besmirched.

Dil Parmar was as appalled as we were. Strictly speaking, as letting agent for the Parade, it's up to him to move that rogue on. He has promised to do so.

To calm my nerves, I took Jean to lunch at Grants. It wasn't exactly overflowing. Now that the menu's in place, I'm beginning to have my doubts about it. I can't believe cheese in filo pastry or wild mushrooms hail from either Italy or California. As for squid in it's own ink, there can't be any call for that sort of thing in any country. In all honesty, I think I preferred the old fare. At least you knew where you stood with the best of British cuisine.

Jean used the occasion to renew her complaints about our stay-at-home lifestyle. Perhaps Bath will go some way to curing her wanderlust. If not, we'll have to come up on the Lottery. We didn't win a bean this week.

3rd October 1995

I caught Ron in a foul mood this morning. He launched into a tirade about Dil Parmar's failure to move Jimmy Corkhill on. I came in for some flak, too, for not doing more. There's nothing I can do. I've gone through the regulations with a fine-toothed comb, but as far as I can see, he's acting legally.

As for using reason, that's failed miserably. I felt a little guilty about not helping Ron out, so I had another go at negotiating with Corkhill. I might as well have been talking to Cracker for all the good it did. The only ray of hope is that he's actively seeking new premises. Until then, he won't budge an inch. Dil Parmar told me he'd had a very similar conversation. Ron will simply have to put up with it. I can only hope he doesn't decide to do something drastic.

5th October 1995

We're off to Bath tomorrow. Making sure all is prepared has been a major organizational headache, however. I spent the last two days working out contingency plans for the B.R.A. to cover my absence from the community this week. Max now has a precise emergency proforma about procedure. I devised a flow chart, showing who has responsibility for what, which authorities should be informed and where any necessary tools and equipment are. Even if World War Three were to break out, the residents of Brookside Close wouldn't be caught completely flat-footed.

Rachel was another problem. I arranged for her to stay with Patricia as Mandy and Sinbad are still enjoying themselves in the Lakes. However, the womenfolk decided to go against my plans. Rachel insisted on staying at the bungalow by herself and Jean backed her up. Once those two get it into their heads to be obstinate, there's no shifting them. It means that I'm sitting here at midnight, surrounded by packing cases, having to make up yet another list.

1. Make sure all the windows and doors are secure.
2. Contact Max if there are any problems with locks, etc.
3. Lottery money to Eddie Banks.
4. Milk money to milkman.
5. Please record *The Archers* and *Crimewatch*.

7th October 1995

Bath.

We've won! We've actually done it!!

THE LOTTERY IS OURS.

I can't quite take it in. There I was, sitting in front of

the television, checking the numbers off. Jean was talking to me through the bathroom door and I only had half my mind on it. I suppose one always watches in that way, half hoping the numbers will come up, but hardly expecting it. When the first was ticked off, I barely noticed. It got to three and the prospect of a tenner proved pleasing.

Four.

Five.

And the bonus.

This is the big one. We're rich. Really rich. Our futures are secure. We need never fear old age again.

Our first move was a bottle of vintage champagne. We spent the evening planning how to spend our winnings over oysters, caviare and lobster. Unsurprisingly, Jean's mind ran to impractical visits to foreign parts. All the money in the world won't buy luxury in the places she wants to go. For myself, I made a list of things we really need. Must remember to add new gardening tools. We'll share our good fortune with Max and Patricia, of course, not to mention Rachel. She's practically family now and she was the one who handed over our stake.

We tried to phone the Banks when we got back, but there was no reply. No doubt they were celebrating. Rachel wasn't in either. We won't know the exact amount until Eddie and Rosie get home, but I'm confident it's going to be a pretty tidy sum.

10th October 1995

We got home this morning to find the house empty. Jean started making an itinerary for her world trip, while I unpacked. I refrained from pointing out that at her age, it's hardly dignified to clamber up mountains on a donkey.

Rachel got back about an hour later. She didn't seem exactly over the moon at our good fortune and when we finally got in touch with the Banks, we found out why. The entire family drove up in a hideous 4x4 monstrosity. It's far too big for their drive and totally inappropriate for driving around Liverpool.

Naturally, when we spotted them, Jean and I rushed out, champagne in hand. Then Eddie let us in on the horrible truth. Rachel forgot to hand over our £2. Instead of realizing a mix-up had occurred, Rosie and Eddie assumed the syndicate was off. They'd put in their money and claimed one hundred thousand pounds for themselves.

I couldn't believe my ears. Surely they can't do that. We had a verbal agreement. A contract. It's outrageous. Our dreams destroyed in an instant. Poor Jean burst into floods of tears.

We're entitled to half of that money. Eddie flatly refused to hand it over, although Rosie had the grace to look embarrassed. There was nothing we could do in the middle of the Close, but this isn't the end of the matter by any means.

13th October 1995

At least, somebody has had some good news. Sinbad telephoned last night to announce the arrival of a baby daughter. Mother and child are doing well and will be out of hospital very soon. Rachel is delighted with her new sister, whom she wishes to name Eternity. What sort of name is that for a human being? Luckily, Sinbad and Mandy have not been swayed. The child is Ruth Elizabeth, after Sinbad's mother and poor Beth. Excellent choices. You can't go wrong with two Biblical names.

Sinbad's as proud as Punch of his fianceé and his daughter. I'm so glad things are working out for him at last. He told me Mandy is really putting the past behind her. She meant what she said when the Appeal Court freed her about helping other battered women. The woman who runs the refuge that rescued her asked her to get in touch with a young woman in need of support. Apparently, this Cathy is being systematically bullied and beaten by a brute of a husband, to such an extent that she's terrified to leave. Mandy wrote her experiences to her in the hope it would encourage her to make the break.

I only wish Jean and my good fortune would come home to roost. The Banks won't budge about the Lottery money. We've tried reasoning and even pleading with them, to no avail. The news has slipped out. Personally, I regret this, as I'm not one to gossip. On the other hand, perhaps the neighbours do have a right to be informed of the perfidy of two of their number.

I've been trying to gauge public opinion. An overwhelming majority seem to believe that not only are the Banks morally indefensible, but legally wrong too. Even Jimmy Corkhill put in his two penn'orth. I'm not sure that having him as an ally will be entirely productive. He suggested making Rosie and Eddie see sense with a baseball bat. That's all we need. Corkhill sending the heavy mob round to the Banks. We have not got to that stage yet. If the worst comes to the worst, we shall simply have to take legal action.

18th October 1995

I have had to admit defeat on the Corkhill front. While we were away, his revolting caravan disappeared, only to be replaced this morning by a Portakabin. Admittedly, it's less of an eyesore and its presence by the petrol station is not causing quite such an obstruction. Naturally, I used my official position to insist on seeing Corkhill's document. They were all in order. The idea of a cowboy like him running a business on our very doorstep makes my gorge rise, but there's nothing I can do about it now.

This is not the case with the lottery money. Jean decided a subtle approach was called for and invited Rosie and Eddie round to dinner. The idea was for the four of us to get round the negotiating table and discuss the matter like adults. I wasn't happy about it from the beginning. After the way they'd treated us, I was uncomfortable with them in the house. I knew the whole exercise would prove to be fruitless. Eddie's as stubborn as a mule. Why would he suddenly start playing fair and square because we provide him with a spot of supper? However, I've always respected Jean's optimism and once she makes up her mind, there's no dissuading her.

It was an appalling evening. The bolognaise turned to dust in my mouth as we discussed the intricacies of the weather to avoid getting to the point. Over coffee, the cards were slung on to the table. I made our position quite clear. We've been treated most unfairly. They had no right to assume the syndicate was off. If it had been the other way round, we'd have put the money in for them. You can't just cancel an agreement like that. How were we to know that Rachel would forget to pass the stake on?

Jean appealed to their compassion. We're not getting any younger. The chances of us coming across that kind of money again are minuscule. We'll never be able to do what we want now. Could they not put themselves in our shoes for a moment?

No, they couldn't. They were open to neither guilt nor legal arguments. Eddie was the problem. I could see Rosie visibly wavering. She has a good heart, but Eddie refuses to compromise. I can't believe the audacity of the man. He even used the numbers that I had carefully selected. Surely that proves the syndicate was a proper arrangement.

Eddie refused to budge. In the end, voices were raised

and he stalked out. However, I have a few ideas up my sleeve. I will not admit defeat yet.

20th October 1995

I popped over to the Banks' to hand over our stake for tomorrow's draw, as this would prove the syndicate is still operating. Eddie got in a panic and refused to accept it. I then insisted he choose different numbers and the wretch slammed the door in my face.

Two hours later, the doorbell rang and there were two shamefaced neighbours holding out an olive branch in the form of a bundle of banknotes. Success, I thought. Only the branch proved to be more of a twig. Five hundred pounds they offered us. A mere one per cent of our rightful winnings. What about the other £49,500? I have never felt so insulted in my life. Jean came to the door to back me up and adamantly refused to accept such a paltry offering. I flung the money back in Eddie's smug face. He failed to catch it and tenners blew all over the Close. Rosie and Eddie spent a good half hour scrabbling on the ground, trying to pick them up. Which just about sums the situation up.

24th October 1995

Things are hotting up. The Banks are being ostracized. Sinbad is refusing to wash their windows and Rachel told me Lee has told his parents how disgusted he is with them ripping us off.

I went down to the Citizens Advice Bureau to check our legal position. The chappie there told me we don't stand much of a chance. There's no written agreement, so it would be our word against the Banks'. We've got no proof that a syndicate was in operation. If we go to court, we'd probably lose *and* face enormous legal costs.

We're not beaten yet, though. I thought it was time to be a little flexible with the truth. See if I can't tie the Banks in knots with a bit of legal red tape. Blind them with science, as it were.

I went round and informed them my solicitor considered we have an excellent case. I mentioned a fictitious case heard in the civil courts last month. I threatened immediate legal action. That should smoke them out.

25th October 1995

No word from Eddie and Rosie. Young Lee is getting caught in the crossfire, though. Patricia asked Rachel to babysit this evening. Rachel invited Lee to go with her, but Patsy, bless her loyal heart, refused to have him in the house. Perhaps the Banks will pay heed to the torment of their child. Surely they can't hold out against everyone's ill will for long.

Rachel went to visit Ruth Elizabeth, who is a delightful bundle of joy. It's amazing how much confidence Mandy is gaining. Not only is she coping with a new baby, she's found time to help this Cathy escape from her husband. There are drawbacks to this kind of work, though. The husband actually turned up on the doorstep, demanding to know of Cathy's whereabouts. Sinbad came home to find him threatening Mandy and slung him out.

Mandy has announced she doesn't want to be 'just a housewife' all her life. It seems there's a job going in the refuge. Sinbad came round to talk it over. Mandy's turned the post down, as it's women only. He's not convinced it's the best decision for her. The man has a heart of gold, willing to sacrifice himself for the happiness of the one he loves.

30th October 1995

I can't believe it. The Banks had a change of heart. Just as Jean and I had completely given up hope. As the days ticked by, we realized the threat of legal action hadn't worked and it was time to bring the unseemly business to a conclusion. We'd have won a moral, if not a financial victory.

We set off across the Close to let them know we were withdrawing our claim. The two couples met in the middle. Rosie simply held out the £50,000 and said they'd had a change of heart. No more explanation than that. Then she apologized, saying they'd been a bit hasty.

What could we do but accept both apology and cash

with grace? It's all there. every last penny. Rachel's theory is that they couldn't cope with being ignored by the community. Whatever it is, I'm glad they've recovered the moral high ground at last.

The three of us spent a blissful evening planning how to spend it. Jean, unsurprisingly, is heading straight for the travel agent. Personally, new tea towels are the first item on my agenda. Then a spot of redecorating is in order. I feel strongly that we ought to be a little more frugal with our windfall. It won't last if we spend it needlessly.

5th November 1995

I came home to find a large atlas pinned up in the living room. Using a variety of map pins and tatty bits of wool, Jean has plotted her route around the world. She's really going through with it, whatever I decided to do. Her ticket's paid for and she plans to be away for some months. She's even bought herself a Tibetan hat, complete with ear-flaps and tassels. It makes her look like a superannuated Sherpa.

I fear she'll be going on her own. At my time of life, it's far too late to become a hobo. I prefer the comfort of my own bed, although I could be tempted into a couple of weeks cruising in the Caribbean. Anything else is out of the question. Some of the ships look absolutely extraordinary. More like floating hotels these days. I rather fancy an en suite jacuzzi.

How can Jean be so pig-headed? I can't believe she really wants to go ahead with all this nonsense. Journey in search of enlightenment indeed! A journey in search of an early grave, more like. I don't think the authorities should allow it for someone of her age.

I'd almost forgotten it was Guy Fawkes night, until I was harassed for £1 for the guy by a gaggle of spotty youngsters. Whilst Jean and I were bickering over the proper way to globetrot, Mandy came to say goodbye. Just like that. She realized she couldn't settle for ordinary family life after all she's been through. With Sinbad's full backing, she's decided to take the job at the refuge. He'll be able to visit his daughter whenever he likes, of course. But it appeared to be the end for this luckless couple.

Do I have the same courage to let Jean follow her dream? She's wanted this adventure for as long as I've known her. And she'll be coming back. In a few months, we'll be reunited. Sinbad and Mandy will probably never be together now.

Mandy and Rachel spent a long time together, saying goodbye. Rachel's grown up so suddenly. She accepts her mother's leaving and is proud of her. I'm sure she'll visit as often as she can. Jean and I promised we'd look after Rachel for her as if she was our own.

Very quietly, with no fuss, Mandy left Liverpool forever. If we'd known in advance, we could have organized a send-off for her, but perhaps she preferred to slip off into the night. As the taxi pulled away from the Close, a huge display of fireworks burst overhead.

Rachel, Jean and I stood on the doorstep for hours watching the celebrations.

As I write this I can't help but feel that today is the end of an important chapter in my life. With Mandy moving on, Jean determined to do her Sherpa Tensing impersonation and Rachel growing up into a fine, young, independent woman, I think it's time to purchase a new desk diary. Of course, I intend to archive this tome, in the hope that I can attract a suitable publisher to put my work into print so the world can share in this most extraordinary section of my life.

BROOKSIDE: THE EARLY YEARS

* Revised and updated edition of the original *Brookside: The First Ten Years*

* Publication to coincide with the transmission of **'Brookside: The Early Years'** on UK Living

* Chronicles the background of the series, its original aims and its evolution over the first decade

* Includes a month-by-month plot summary of the first ten years

* All the characters are featured – from the Grants and the Collinses to the Corkhills and the Dixons

* Individual profiles of the characters and interviews with the cast members

* Illustrated with photographs of the characters and memorable moments from the early years

Geoff Tibballs
0 7522 1051 3
£7.99 pb

SPECIAL ORDER FORM

TV TIE INS

1 85283 959 7	Emmerdale Family Album	£9.99 pb
1 85283 964 3	The Bill: The First Ten Years	£4.99 pb
0 7522 0663 X	Harvey Moon's Memoirs Vol 2	£14.99 hb
0 7522 0736 9	Roughnecks	£14.99 pb

BROOKSIDE

1 85283 954 6	Phil Redmond's Brookside: Life in the Close	£9.99 pb
0 7522 0972 8	The Journals of Beth Jordache	£4.99 pb
0 7522 0765 2	Beth Jordache The New Journals	£4.99 pb
0 7522 0846 2	The Jimmy Corkhill Story	£4.99 pb
0 7522 1051 3	The Early Years	£7.99 pb

CORONATION STREET

1 85283 464 1	The Coronation Street Story	£16.99 hb
1 85283 456 0	Life and Times of Rovers Return	£14.99 hb
0 7522 0197 2	Coronation Street Quiz Book	£3.50 pb

LONDON'S BURNING

1 85283 874 4	London's Burning	£9.99 pb
0 7522 1085 8	London's Burning: Behind the Blaze	£14.99 hb

SOLDIER, SOLDIER

1 85283 480 3	Soldier, Soldier	£9.99 pb
0 7522 1055 6	Soldier, Soldier – The Regiment Files	£14.99 hb
0 7522 0750 4	Soldier, Soldier Novelisation: Tucker's Story	£4.99 pb
0 7522 0755 5	Soldier, Soldier Novelisation: Damage	£4.99 pb

All these books are available at your local bookshop or can be ordered direct from the publisher. Just tick the titles you want and fill in the form below.

Prices and availability subject to change without notice.

Boxtree Cash Sales, P.O. Box 11, Falmouth, Cornwall TR10 9EN

Please send a cheque or postal order for the value of the book and add the following for postage and packing:

U.K. including B.F.P.O. – £1.00 for one book plus 50p for the second book, and 30p for each additional book ordered up to a £3.00 maximum.

Overseas including Eire – £2.00 for the first book plus £1.00 for the second book, and 50p for each additional book ordered.

OR please debit this amount from my Access/Visa Card (delete as appropriate).

Card Number | | | | | | | | | | | | | | | | |

Amount £ ....

Expiry Date ....

Signed ....

Name ....

Address ....

....

....